CORPSE
ON
THE COURT

CORPSE
ON
THE COURT

•

Deborah Tisdale

AVALON BOOKS
NEW YORK

PRINTED IN THE UNITED STATES OF AMERICA
ON ACID-FREE PAPER
BY HADDON CRAFTSMEN, BLOOMSBURG, PENNSYLVANIA

This book is dedicated to my dad,
Jeff Tisdale,
one of the best storytellers I've ever known.

Thanks so much to my editor, Erin Cartwright, who encouraged and guided me through my first mystery novel. Without her editorial direction, I never could have done it.

I'd like to thank ex-officer, Lynda Cooper, and her police officer husband, Trent, for sharing with me what cops would and wouldn't do in certain "sticky" situations.

I also need to thank East Lake Woodlands Chief of Security, Charlie Thornton, fellow writer, Denise Camp, and all the Pinellas County deputies I stopped to question about procedures.

Chapter One

When I left the Nashville Police Department, I swore I'd never be involved with law enforcement again for as long as I lived. And I meant it. At the time.

For the past twelve years, I've been everything from a patrol officer to a desk sergeant, and then right before I left, a detective—homicide, my specialty. It was not that I didn't thoroughly enjoy the grisly scenes I saw on a weekly basis, it's just that I was beginning to feel like my life wasn't normal. I wanted to be normal—whatever that was.

I didn't know exactly why I had to leave, but I did know one thing: I was burned out. I had nothing left to give.

I knew that I'd have to start over in some new career, but I was willing to take a huge cut in pay, and I figured the sacrifice would be worth it. My heart wouldn't sink every time I heard the wail of a siren, fearing I was about to be called in to go view a murder scene and then do a report without losing my lunch. Now, when I spotted something suspicious, I could either call 911 or if it wasn't too bad, I could do what most people did—turn my head the other way. And I'd be able to watch my favorite cop shows on television without screaming at the screen that they were doing it all wrong. I'd be able to sit and enjoy the program for a change.

After my going-away party, I walked out of that precinct station with a smile so wide my cheeks burned. Sure, I'd miss my buddies, but I knew I could always meet them for lunch sometime, at least until I decided what I wanted to do with the rest of my life.

But for now, I was content knowing that I'd be spending the next few weeks down in Florida, recharging my mental and emotional batteries, hanging out with my Uncle Bing, a man whose only goal in life was to score with the most recently widowed woman in the development. No, Bing isn't his real name, but he always liked the crooner Bing Crosby, so he gave himself that nickname and it stuck. I can't say I blame him, it's better than the name John Smith he'd been given by unimaginative parents.

Bing lives in a condo overlooking the ninth green of Gulfside Country Club, one of many planned suburban developments owned by the mighty conglomerate, Crestview Country Club Communities. This company had earned the reputation of moving into areas and turning cheap land into expensive property by sticking a golf course on it, which was what had happened in Gulfside. The development where Uncle Bing lived was once nothing but swampland with all the creatures who still called this place home.

Not that I mind alligators, mosquitoes, and fish I can't name, but I would rather have invested my money in land that didn't squish thick, black mud up over your shoes when you walked on it. But my visit with Uncle Bing was temporary, and I was determined to enjoy it.

"Summer," he said in his raspy voice as he opened the door, "come on in. I've got some iced tea in the kitchen."

Uncle Bing always had iced tea. I'm surprised his kidneys hadn't either withered or exploded, as much tea as this man drank. Offering a tired grin, I shook my head. "I think I'll just put my stuff in the guest room and rest for a few minutes. Where do you want to go for dinner tonight?"

I'd visited with my elderly uncle several times before and we'd established a nice little routine. Every other night he cooked dinner for me. On the other nights, I treated him to dinner out since he was such a willing host. Of course, he liked to go to places he wouldn't have been able to afford without the use of my credit card. But I didn't mind. He was letting me vacation in his condo for free.

Uncle Bing's condo was probably the cheapest way for him to live so close to what he loved—the golf course. The community where he lived offered housing in all price ranges, starting at "unbelievably low, slashed to rock-bottom prices for condos," according to the signs leading to the development to "exquisite luxury executive homes on estate sized lots."

The condos were cheap, pre-fab, two-story structures with lots of what realtors call gingerbread on the surface to make them appealing. The luxury homes were cheap, pre-fab, two-story structures with even more gingerbread, making them attractive to those who didn't know any better so they could feel like they were living the life of Riley.

The community offered all sorts of amenities and catered to all economic levels. Bing was proud of where he lived.

I did notice that the recreation facilities were meticulously maintained, something that Uncle Bing pointed out every chance he got. He took extra time showing off "his" golf course. Ever since I can remember, my mother told me the reason he had never gotten married was because golf was his first love. "And no self-respecting woman wants to put up with a man who stays gone all day when he should be with her."

Being an athlete myself, I enjoyed golf and tennis. I also played softball and bowled, but when I was in Gulfside, I did the country club routine and played the sports that were available to me at Uncle Bing's.

"You're the only woman I know who can walk the entire course with me," he once told me. He liked to pretend that he actually enjoyed not taking a cart, saying that was how he got his exercise. But I knew it was probably more of a matter of economics—carts were expensive.

After I put my things away and rested for a half hour, Uncle Bing came to my door and knocked. "Ready for a night out on the town, Summer?" I knew I wouldn't get much rest the first day I was there, but man, I was tired.

I sat up in the bed and rubbed my forehead. Letting out a huge sigh, I swung my legs over the side and slipped my feet back into my shoes. "I'm ready," I replied.

In spite of his overly exuberant oral essays, all about the country club life, Uncle Bing was a wonderful person to be with. His eyes crinkled when he smiled, and he smiled often. He laughed at every joke, no matter how lame it was. Then, he never failed to come back with a tired one of his own. I often thought he would have made a huge hit in vaudeville, but as usual, his timing was off. He was born a few years too late.

We went to the Gulfside Grill, a small restaurant overlooking the Gulf of Mexico. It was a casual little restaurant that served the best grouper sandwiches I'd ever tasted. I was glad he'd chosen it for my first night—I wasn't in the mood to dress up.

"Hey, Bing," a middle-aged, bleached blond waitress said in a fake sultry voice. "Wanna see our specials?" Her penetrating gaze left no doubt what was on her personal list of specials.

Uncle Bing grinned back at the woman and winked.

"We'll just have the grouper sandwiches, Maude. Extra chips."

She tossed her hair over her muscular shoulder and stuck the pencil behind her ear. "Sure thing, Bing," she said as she grabbed the menus and shoved them between the paper napkin holder and the salt shaker. Then, she left our table for the kitchen.

"What was that all about?" I asked, crinkling my nose.

He sighed and shook his head. "Maude and I went to a movie once, and now she thinks we're an item."

I stifled a giggle. "Well, are you?"

Uncle Bing raised one eyebrow, reached for his water glass, and snorted. "Maude's okay, but not my type."

We spent the better part of the next fifteen minutes trying to figure out what his type was. I have to admit, he and I had two different ideas as to what kind of woman he should go for. One thing we did agree on, though, was that he probably needed to remain single, since he had little to no tolerance for anyone else for very long.

"There is one woman, though," he said and looked at me from beneath hooded eyes.

"Oh, yeah?" I asked. "Tell me about her."

With a shrug, Uncle Bing averted my stare. "Her name's Bonita. She's pretty, and I sort of like her."

"And?" I wanted to know more. Uncle Bing had the look of a smitten schoolboy.

"Not much to tell."

"Be careful, Uncle Bing. You know how much of a push-over you can be."

"Yeah, well . . ." he said, then his voice trailed off.

I laughed. We talked about his love life, and I noticed he'd dropped the subject of this Bonita woman he'd mentioned.

Maude arrived with our sandwiches just as we'd decided he needed to back off dating, since he'd just admitted he'd gotten himself in a couple of binds with women lately. Her lipstick was thicker than when she'd taken our order, a fact that both of us noticed. When she walked away, I saw the way she gently swayed her hips. It wasn't a pretty sight, in my opinion, but Uncle Bing's appreciative gaze gave me no doubt that once again, he and I didn't see things the same way.

Uncle Bing silently enjoyed her show, until she stopped at a table on the other side of the restaurant to take someone else's order. "Play any golf lately, Summer?" he asked before he bit into his sandwich.

I shrugged and turned back to face him. "A little, but I plan to do more while I'm here. I hope you got a tee-off time for us tomorrow."

With a twinkle in his eye, he replied, "I did better than that, Summer. I even reserved a cart."

Whoa! Uncle Bing must have come into some money. "Did you win the lottery and not tell me?" I asked with a snort. He'd always told me that carts were for little old ladies.

"No, of course not. Real people never win those things. I just figured that we'd splurge and take a cart.

But only once. After we finish playing nine holes, I thought we could head on over to the tennis courts and knock a few balls around. I didn't want to wear you out."

"Mighty thoughtful of you, Uncle Bing," I said, holding in my thoughts that it wasn't me he was worried about. For the first time since I could remember, he was starting to show his age. He must have been in his early seventies by now. I figured it must be pretty rough for him to walk the entire golf course.

"Yeah," he replied, taking a sip of his tea. "I don't want you to overdo it." He seemed to be finding it hard to look me directly in the eye.

I thought for a moment before I reached out and touched his arm. "Uncle Bing, have you given any consideration to moving back to Tennessee?"

He looked at me as if I'd sprouted a new head. I obviously had his attention with that simple question of concern. "Now why would I want to go and do that?"

With a shrug, I said, "I dunno. Maybe it would be nice for you to be closer to family."

"I like Florida." His chin jutted out, like that of a stubborn three year old.

Uncle Bing was an attractive man, like the classic actors from late-night movies on television. My mom and I used to watch them when I lived at home.

"But what about the people you love? You're not getting any younger, Uncle Bing, in spite of how healthy you've been. Don't you want to be a little closer to family?"

He slammed his glass down, causing ice to jump out of it and onto the table, iced tea pooling around the cubes. "I am *not* getting old," he growled. "And I will *not* leave Florida. This is my home."

I licked my lips and thought for a moment as I nodded. I hadn't meant to offend my favorite uncle. It didn't come out right. I just wanted him to know the family would be there for him if he needed us.

"Yes, I understand," I replied, knowing that I'd have to wait a long time to bring up the subject again. My mom had made me promise to try to talk him into it while I was here, and I may have just blown it. I slowly folded my napkin and put it on the table. "This was an excellent choice for dinner, by the way."

It took him a minute to get over his anger—or hurt feelings, I'm not sure which—but I knew he would. Finally, he smiled at me and nodded. "I've always liked this place. On Saturdays they have a guy playing honky-tonk piano. And they clear a spot on the floor so people can dance. Maybe we can come back." He glanced over his shoulder at Maude, who'd just finished cleaning off another table. There must be something still going on between them, I thought. He'd been awfully interested in where she was, even after he'd acted like he wasn't.

"Sounds good," I replied. "Let's head on back to your place. I'm getting tired."

"Uh, Summer, I need to talk to you about something kind of personal."

"A woman?"

He nodded. "But not now." Handing the keys to me, he said, "You drive."

We didn't say much to each other on the way home. I noticed that Uncle Bing was being more quiet than usual, so I tried to let him have his space. No sense in antagonizing him when he had some thinking to do.

"What the—?" Uncle Bing said, causing me to look up ahead.

There were several police cars lined up in the parking lot, and the property manager was out there talking to a bunch of people. This kind of activity wasn't normal for Uncle Bing's neighborhood.

"Now what do you suppose is going on?" he asked. "Nothing ever happens around this place. Someone must have died."

I frowned. My years being detective in Nashville had done something to my nerves. And it had sharpened my instincts as well. I'd noticed how when one man spotted Uncle Bing's car, he made a comment to the people standing around him. They all turned and watched as we drove up the street. The hair on the back of my neck stood on end. "I think someone might want to talk to you, Uncle Bing," I said softly.

"Now why would you think something like that?" he asked. "I don't have any information they'd want to know."

"Uh, Uncle Bing," I said, pointing to the three uniformed officers that were headed our way. "They definitely want to talk to you."

"I haven't done anything wrong, Summer," he replied. "I swear."

Shaking my head, I squinted and glanced up at his front door. "Someone has put something on your door. Looks like a business card." There was something rectangular and white perched above his door knocker. Yep, I thought, a business card.

He made a harumphing sound. "That don't mean a thing."

I knew better. Whenever I needed to question a witness, I always left my business card if they weren't home or didn't answer the door when I knocked. But I nodded. "I hope you're right," I said.

I pulled his car into the next parking lot over, since his was blocked by police cruisers. "This spot isn't numbered. Is it okay if we park here?"

"Better be," he growled. "The people on this side have parties all the time, and they take up our entire lot without asking."

"And they don't invite you?" I asked.

He made a face. "If they did, do you think I'd be complaining?"

Uncle Bing was a party animal in a colossal way, back in his younger days. I remembered hearing my mother's stories about him when they were growing up. While I listened with feigned shocked interest, I secretly wished my mom could have been more like him. She was the goody-goody in the family, and she expected the same from me.

I'd caused more than my share of trouble for my parents. My father even made the comment once that he'd be happy with anything I did when I grew up as long as I stayed out of jail. I don't know what they thought I was up to, but I was never really that bad. Just a few late parties and broken curfews. No big deal, really.

The looks on their faces were priceless when I came home and informed the family that I'd been accepted into the Nashville Police Academy. "Better a cop than a robber," my dad mumbled, when he was able to pick his chin back up off the floor.

Well, now I knew my training would come in mighty handy. It was obvious that something pretty awful had just happened, and the cops were waiting for someone. Several of the neighbors were standing outside on the front lawn, and they all looked up as they spotted Uncle Bing.

"There he is," one elderly man said, as he blatantly pointed his finger in our direction.

Now that I could actually hear them talking, my heart sank. There were several cruisers and two cars that were very clearly unmarked police cars. I could spot them from a mile away. And so could most crimi-nals, I'd discovered when I had to drive one.

I had no doubt some horrendous crime had been committed, and my uncle was next in line to be inter-viewed. That suspicion was confirmed when a harried looking, middle-aged man started heading toward us, his sleeves rolled up to his elbows, his eyebrows in a permanent arch. I felt like telling him to take a break, but I was afraid he might take some kind of action, based on how he was sizing us up. His movement was apprehensive.

This was worse than I could have imagined, I

thought. My uncle was a suspect in something. I could tell by the way the man was walking toward us and how another cop was standing guard behind one of the cruisers. I knew from experience that he most likely had a gun drawn and was ready to use it if he felt that it was necessary.

"Uh, Uncle Bing," I said through clenched teeth. "Have you been into anything I don't know about lately?"

He looked at me and belted out a hearty chuckle. "You've got quite an imagination, Summer. I haven't done anything more exciting than play golf and tennis since I've been here. Oh, and maybe step out a few times with some of my lady friends." In spite of his attempt at humor, I saw the tension on his face. He knew as well as I did that he was the suspect of some crime, and he was about to be interrogated.

"John Smith?" the cop said, as he got closer. He never took his eyes off Uncle Bing. It was almost like he was afraid we'd do something, like bolt, which we couldn't have, even if we'd wanted to.

Uncle Bing extended his right hand in a gesture of friendship, just like he did to everyone he met. I don't think I've ever met a friendlier person in my life. And I didn't think that cop was in a very friendly mood.

"John Smith's my legal name, but everyone around here calls me Bing."

Until then I didn't think the cop's eyebrows had room to go up anymore, but I was mistaken. Now they were even with his hairline.

He turned his head back and called over his shoulder, "John, alias Bing, Smith." I sure did want to know how he did that. Even though his head was turned at a ninety degree angle, he never once took his eyes off us.

"Got it," the cop with the notepad called back. This one was young, probably right out of the academy.

When the officer coming toward us didn't offer his handshake, Uncle Bing dropped his. "Not very friendly, is he?" he whispered to me. I saw the tremor in Uncle Bing's hand as he pulled it back and stuck it in his pocket.

"Uh, Uncle Bing, I don't think these guys are here to make friends. Just answer their questions and be totally honest." I did my best to keep the worry from showing in my voice, but I was scared half out of my wits for my uncle. He clearly still had no clue, although based on the lines that had deepened around his eyes, I could tell he knew something was up.

"Of course," he said as if I'd hurt his feelings. "I don't know how to be any other way." His voice was tight; he was trying to disguise his concern.

I tried to nudge Uncle Bing to let him know he needed to quit trying to win a popularity contest, but he pulled away. "What happened here?" he asked, joining the group that was standing there, still gawking at him. I inwardly groaned.

"We have a few questions for you, Mr. Smith," the detective told him. "And if you don't mind, we'd like to ask them back at the office."

"Sure thing!" my uncle said. "Just name the time, and I'll be there."

"Now," the officer said, his expression grave.

Uncle Bing grinned and shook his head. "I don't think so, not tonight. My niece just drove in from Nashville, and I think we need to rest. Maybe some other time?"

The two detectives exchanged a glance that I recognized. My uncle was a front line suspect in something, but for some reason they didn't want to arrest him here. The problem was, he still had no clue. My uncle was, without a doubt, the most clueless person I'd ever met.

It was time for me to step forward and try to save the situation. I knew that Uncle Bing was going to the police station, whether he went willingly or not, so it was up to me to get him to cooperate. These guys weren't here for a party.

"Uh, Uncle Bing, I think it might be good if we went with these men," I said softly.

His head whipped around, and he looked at me like I was crazy. "I'm sure that whatever these people want can wait until tomorrow."

The cops all looked back at me to see what I'd say. "No," I replied. "We'd better go now."

"Smart lady," the oldest of the officers said. I thought I might have detected a note of sarcasm in his voice.

Uncle Bing let out a sigh of frustration. "Oh, all right. Wait here. I'll go back and get the car."

"That won't be necessary," the cop in the patrol car said. "You can ride with us."

Uncle Bing grinned, looking like a little boy who'd

just gotten a new video game. "I've always wanted to ride in a cop car." He turned to the police officer and said, "Would you mind turning on the lights and siren?"

The policeman smiled at the detective behind us and nodded. "No problem. I was planning to, anyway."

Chapter Two

I groaned. Was there any way I could get through to him that he was in serious trouble without having to spell it out?

"Sorry, lady," the senior officer said, as I tried to scoot in beside my uncle. He blocked me from getting all the way in. For a moment I thought I might get a ride to the station in the cruiser, but I should have known better. "You'll have to find another way to the station if you wanna join the old man." His voice cracked like that of an adolescent boy.

"Hey," Uncle Bing said as he slid into the back seat of the cruiser. "Watch what you call your elders, young man. I bet I could teach you a thing or two." The cop just shook his head, mumbled a few words I couldn't hear about Uncle Bing's rights, snapped

17

handcuffs on Uncle Bing's wrists, secured the door lock, and quickly moved around to the driver's side.

I chewed my lip as Uncle Bing was whisked away in the patrol car, sirens blaring, the blue light swirling. When they were out of sight, I turned and saw how the whole community had shown up for the big spectacle. It was obvious that Uncle Bing was in his element in this place. As I looked out over the sea of gray heads with an occasional dye job, I saw that no one was younger than at least sixty-five, and even that was a young guess. My uncle was most likely one of the youngest ones there. Quite unlike Nashville, where the Gen-Xer country music star wannabes seemed to rule the town, driving around in pickup trucks with Shania Twain music blasting from woofers designed for a coliseum.

All eyes were on me, like they were waiting for a confession, or something. I still had no idea what was going on, but I was about to find out. As much as I'd wanted to quit being a detective, I now had a reason to continue. Uncle Bing needed me in the worst kind of way.

I sucked in a deep breath and slowly blew it out. Two of the women who stood in the background began to whisper behind cupped hands, something I'd been taught was very rude. Their eyes darted around, like they were trying to hide the fact that they were talking about me. One of them even smiled, obviously trained in the fine art of gossip.

Finally, I took a step toward the crowd. "Anyone

here have an idea why my uncle was hauled away by the cops?"

As I moved toward them, several of the ladies took one step back. The few men who were there didn't seem intimidated by me, but they weren't forthcoming with information either. However, after a brief hesitation, one man actually came closer. "Old lady in 7-B was murdered today. She was found strangled, face down on the tennis court."

"Murdered?" I said, my voice cracking. Surely, Uncle Bing couldn't be a suspect in a murder case. Maybe he was being called as a witness. But somehow in the back of my mind, I knew that wasn't the case. Cops didn't snap handcuffs on mere witnesses.

"Yeah, missy," he said in an almost mocking manner, making me wish I was still a cop so I could instill a little respect in him. "Bonita Landry and Bing had a thing goin', and they think he might have killed her. Rumor has it she's been hot after some other guy, and Bing couldn't handle it."

The name Bonita rang through my mind. That's the woman Uncle Bing mentioned at dinner.

The first time I opened my mouth to talk, a faint squeak came out. I had to clear my throat and try again.

"You mean to tell me you all just stood there and watched my Uncle Bing get hauled away by the cops without saying anything?" These *were* his friends, weren't they? "Surely you don't think he did it."

The man who'd taken another step closer to me

nodded and grinned. "What makes you think he's innocent?"

I narrowed my eyes and glared at him, silently daring him to take another step. His face twitched, and he stopped his forward momentum. He'd gotten my message.

Using my police-trained voice, I growled, "Who are you, anyway?"

He nervously reached up and twisted his mustache between his thumb and forefinger. A slow chuckle resounded from his throat, then he belted out a rip-roaring laugh. "I'm Clyde Bullhouser, the president of this condo association."

"President, huh?" I said, keeping my tone as level as I could, letting my police training take over. At least I wouldn't come undone as I asked a few questions of this peculiar fellow. "So I suppose you probably know everyone in this building."

Mr. Bullhouser nodded. "Yes, ma'am, I most certainly do. In fact, I won the last election by a landslide."

"I'm sure you did," I said offhandedly, kicking my brain into high gear to quickly assess the situation. Everyone was still standing outside, staring at me as if they expected me to do something. And Mr. Bullhouser was clearly the only person who was willing to speak out. At least at the moment.

He snorted. "That womanizing uncle of yours tried to run against me, but his lady-killing lines weren't enough to send him to the top." His chest was pumped, and he was strutting around the parking lot like a barn-yard rooster.

"No, I guess they weren't," I replied, glancing back at him. There was something in the way he spoke of my uncle that made me wonder what was going on in his head. He took a little too much pleasure from Uncle Bing's plight. I went on instinct. "You weren't, by any chance, involved with this Bonita Landry, were you?"

Mr. Bullhouser nervously looked around and took another step toward me. All ears remained tuned in to our discussion; in fact, most people had actually leaned closer. He turned and scowled at the crowd. "Go back inside, everyone. Show's over." Then, he turned back to me. "How long you in town, Miss Walsh?"

Alarm bells went off in my mind. How did this man know my last name? I was related to Uncle Bing on my mom's side of the family, so we didn't share the same last name. I didn't see any reason for him to know anything about me, especially given the fact that he and my uncle weren't exactly the best of friends.

With the tingling sensation at the nape of my neck and my guard rising even higher, I stared directly at him. "As long as I need to be."

Watching the man's Adam's apple dip beneath his polo shirt as he swallowed hard, I knew he had something up his sleeve. In fact, he was acting mighty guilty about something. I held back my contempt, knowing that if this Mr. Bullhouser had something I needed, I'd have to remain neutral.

"I suppose you'll want to stick around and see what happens to your uncle, huh?" he finally said.

"Yes," I replied, "I suppose I will."

Mr. Bullhouser turned to the side and began to edge toward the building. "I best be gettin' inside and get some rest. Tomorrow will be here before we know it."

"Wait a minute," I said in my best cop voice.

He turned and faced me head-on once again, a look of utter surprise on his face. I could only imagine how shocked he was at how demanding I could sound.

"What is it now?" he asked, his voice dripping with impatience.

"How do I get to the police station?"

Mr. Bullhouser laughed nervously, glancing at his obviously fake Rolex that was a little too shiny. "Don't tell me you're gonna go there at this hour."

That was exactly what I planned to do. "I *am* going there at this hour, and you're gonna take me."

"I don't think so, Miss Walsh." He turned his back to me and began walking toward the building, leaving me standing alone in the parking lot. I knew everyone was watching from their windows because no lights were on in the condos and curtains moved on the other sides of unopened windows.

"If you don't, then I'll have to find it by myself," I said, making him think I'd accepted his decision to drop the issue. Then, just as his guard was down, I called out, "But you might want to stay up a little while longer because when I get there, I'm sure they'll be interested in my story about how you and my uncle were fighting over Ms. Landry before she died."

He spun around and faced me once again. "What?" he shrieked.

With a cake-eating grin, I nodded. "Framing another man for your crime will only get you into more trouble, Mr. Bullhouser." I'd always wanted to spout off an accusation without sufficient evidence like that, but when I was an official cop, the department wouldn't allow it. Now that I was a civilian, I could say anything I pleased and not have to worry about it holding up in court.

The only light came from the streetlights, and I couldn't see the color of his face, so I could only imagine the blood draining from it as he stopped in his tracks. "I didn't murder Bonita, Miss Walsh," he said. "And I didn't frame your uncle."

I shrugged. "We'll just have to see what the cops think when I tell them what you just told me about how you were worried about my uncle beating you out of the presidency." This sounded so juvenile, yet it was the most serious thing I'd ever encountered personally while not on duty. Besides, it seemed to fit the occasion.

"I didn't say that," he said, his voice still shrill from disbelief.

"Maybe not, but I can read between the lines. You and Ms. Landry had quite a thing going before my uncle managed to woo her away from you. Too bad you don't have his charm, Mr. Bullhouser."

He let out a deep sigh and shook his head. "Okay, I'll take you to the police station, Miss Walsh. Just don't start crying and getting all weepy over your uncle on the way there. He's in trouble on account of his own hot head, and there's nothing I can do about it."

"Maybe not, Mr. Bullhouser," I said in my most southern-belle tone, "but I have a feeling you might carry a little clout around here."

The man actually puffed out his chest again and grinned with pride. Man, was he an easy one to manipulate! "Yes, I do have some say in what happens around this place. That's why I'm the president."

Either Clyde Bullhouser was the clever murderer of the woman who'd been strangled on the tennis court or he was the biggest buffoon I'd ever met. I needed to study him a little longer before I could draw a firm conclusion. In the meantime, I needed to figure out a way to get Uncle Bing out of the jail cell he was probably occupying right now. He'd been with the cops long enough for them to get sufficient information to put him behind bars, at least temporarily. Even though I still had no doubt of his innocence, I knew how he liked to boast, which to some ears would sound like a confession.

As we drove to the police station in Clyde Bullhouser's land yacht, I got a lesson on the history of his condo association. Most of the information was irrelevant, but it kept silence from shrouding the car. Clyde Bullhouser was full of himself, and he wanted me to hear all his attributes. He'd been one of the first buyers in this particular building, and he was instrumental in forming a separate association from the rest of the development. "We have a completely different set of problems from the people in single family homes," he said in a very serious tone, as if that was the most important thing in his life at the moment. "First of all, they don't have neighbors living on top or beneath them."

"Yeah," I answered in agreement, only half listening.

"So I found an attorney who drew up the documents to form our association. Did I tell you what the name of our association is?" he asked.

I let out an exasperated breath. "No, I don't believe you did."

"Condos on the Green," he said proudly. "Has a nice ring, doesn't it?"

I nodded as my mind wandered. "Yes, very nice." *Was Uncle Bing read his rights?* I wondered. *Would he, in his clueless innocence, have blown his defense by saying something inane, trying to charm the investigators?* I wished I'd known he was going to be questioned about a murder before he'd left, or I would have insisted on talking to him first.

As we got out of the car, I felt a brisk breeze whip up from the west. The moist, salty air had already frizzed my hair beyond recognition, and my clothes were sticking to my body. How Uncle Bing could stand living in such a miserably damp climate was beyond me. But he seemed to love it. While I enjoyed vacationing in Florida, the thought of living here didn't appeal to me in the least.

"Here we are, Miss Walsh," he said as he pulled

into the parking lot on the side of the police station. "I'll go inside with you to make sure you're okay."

"That's mighty nice of you," I said sarcastically. But I don't think he caught my sardonic tone. He just grinned at me like he thought I might actually believe his motives were purely to watch over me.

"Old Bing wouldn't appreciate it if I let his niece out on the dark streets of Gulfside," he continued. "A girl like you needs someone to look after her."

I almost choked. Mr. Bullhouser obviously didn't know much about me, besides my name. Uncle Bing was just as ashamed of my being a cop as everyone else in the family. I wanted to tell Mr. Bullhouser that I was the one who'd do the protecting if anyone messed with us, but I seriously doubted much would happen in Gulfside, no matter what time it was.

Then, I thought about what we were here for—the murder. Even Gulfside was changing.

The woman at the front desk didn't even glance up when we entered the lobby. "First door to the right," she said in a monotone pointing to a hallway off to the side of the room. Then, she let out a low giggle. "Nice to see you again, Clyde."

I tossed a questioning glance to Mr. Bullhouser. He shrugged and motioned for me to follow him.

As we walked down the short hall, I tried hard not to inhale too deeply. The blended smell of ammonia and carbon copies reminded me of what I'd left behind. At least the walls here were painted yellow rather than the stark gray of the Nashville police department. While I would have gagged if I'd had to look at this place day in and day out, it wasn't too bad to have to face it now.

When we got to the door, Mr. Bullhouser hesitated and looked down at me. He was scared. I could tell. Oh well, I suppose anyone would be in a situation like this. I lifted my fist and knocked. A deep, masculine voice said, "Not now, Eunice. I'm finishing up my report."

"Uh, Captain Stokes, sir," I said, assuming the name on the door belonged to the man inside the office, "I'm Summer Walsh, and I'm here to inquire about my uncle, John Smith."

There was a brief silence and hesitation before I heard the sound of heels clicking on the linoleum floor. The door swung open, and I found myself standing face to face with a man about my height, thirty-something, dark brown hair, light brown eyes, and wearing a weary expression. "Sorry," he said, taking a step back. "We don't get many visitors during my shift. Won't you come in?" He curiously glanced at Mr. Bullhouser.

"He's with me. A neighbor of my uncle's," I said, as I marched into the small office.

"What can I do for you?" he asked, shutting the door. "We've already questioned your uncle, and he's here for the night."

I leveled my gaze on him and waited until he started squirming before I began my interrogation. I'd obviously had much better intimidation training than he'd had, so I knew I had the upper hand. Even Mr. Bullhouser was impressed, I could tell. His look was priceless. He still didn't know I'd been a cop.

"Did you read him his rights?" I asked, never once looking away.

"Uh, yes," he said, glancing over his shoulder at something on his desk. "I believe we did."

I nodded, itching to see what he was looking at. But I never took my eyes off him. "Did you inform him of his right to an attorney?"

"Of course, we did," he replied. "But he said he didn't need one. Said he's innocent."

"You did record your interrogation, right?" I asked, arching my brows, letting him know I was savvy.

He crinkled his forehead, glanced over at Mr. Bullhouser, then looked back at me. "Of course, we did."

"Did he say anything to incriminate himself?"

"Well, not yet, he didn't." The captain shook his head as he continued. "We're not finished with him, though. In the meantime, we have to hold him here to protect the citizens of Gulfside."

"Protect the citizens from my uncle?" I shrieked. That was the most ridiculous thing I'd ever heard in my life.

Uncle Bing *was* innocent. I knew it in my bones. But I could also tell that this cop assumed my uncle's guilt. I had to pull out all the stops.

One thing I'd noticed was that this Captain Stokes hadn't said anything about having arrested Uncle Bing. In fact, he'd been avoiding the word "arrest."

Taking a step forward, putting myself almost directly in the guy's face, I said, "What grounds do you have for keeping my uncle here overnight?"

Chapter Three

Captain Stokes let out a nervous snicker and darted his eyes over to my escort, who had actually stood by my side through this whole thing, alternating between shock and amusement. I could tell he was enjoying every moment of this, now that he'd gotten over his initial case of nerves.

"We have plenty of evidence that he's guilty," the cop said. "Now if you'll please go on home now and get a good night's rest, I'm sure you'll have a chance to talk to your uncle tomorrow after we're finished with him."

He had to be joking, I thought. A good night's rest?

"After you're finished with him, my uncle won't know whether he's coming or going," I said, making sure I made myself clear. "So I want to see him now."

"I'm sorry," he said, still snickering and snorting like he had some sort of private joke, "but that's not possible." Then, he actually had the nerve to reach out and try to guide me to the door. But I dug in my heels.

I folded my arms across my chest and planted my feet shoulder width to show him I meant business. "I'm not going anywhere until I see my uncle."

Captain Stokes let out a frustrated breath and raked his fingers through his hair. "You can't."

"And why not?" I asked, holding my stance.

"Your uncle is in jail," he said slowly, as if I were a three year old who wouldn't listen.

"For him to be in jail, you had to have arrested him."

Nodding, Captain Stokes smiled, as if we'd finally gotten the point. "Yes, he's been arrested."

"What's the charge?" I asked, still not budging.

The man actually rolled his eyes. "Murder."

"What grounds?" Repeating questions was the best way to trip someone up, I remembered.

Captain Stokes started pacing, sucking in breath, blowing it out like a whale, and rubbing his neck. I was getting to him. Good.

"C'mon, Summer," Mr. Bullhouser said, reaching out to tug my elbow.

I yanked my arm away from him and turned back to face the cop. "Answer me, Captain. Did you have a warrant?"

"Of course, we had a warrant," he growled.

I'd been hoping that the slip-up would be basic, so this whole thing could be over with, but they'd managed to cover themselves with a warrant. I had to take it a step further.

"On what grounds did you get the warrant?" I asked.

"Lady, you've been watching too many cop shows. Someone needs to keep you in touch with reality," Captain Stokes said as he crossed the room and sat back down at his desk. "Now if you'll please excuse me, I have work to do."

The last few statements he made took my anger to a new level. Until this point, all he was doing was annoying me, but now I wanted to hang him. Again, I had to yank my arm free from Clyde Bullhouser to follow the captain over to his desk. I leaned forward to where my face was inches from his. In the lowest growl I was able to make, I said, "For the past twelve years, I haven't watched many cop shows. In fact, I've been so busy being a real cop, I haven't had much time for anything. Now I want you to be a real cop and let me see my uncle, and if you continue denying me access, I'll keep going until I find some little 'T' you forgot to cross. And then you'll be sorry you said what you just said."

The room suddenly grew so silent, I could hear the rumble in Mr. Bullhouser's stomach. At least now I had the upper hand, even if it was borne of their shock. The room grew so quiet you could hear a pin drop.

After a long moment of silence, Captain Stokes mumbled, "You're a cop? Where?"

I tilted my head back and groaned. Now he wanted to talk shop, which would have been just fine if my uncle hadn't been sitting in a jail cell for the past hour or so.

Letting out another breath of frustration, I blurted, "Nashville." Then, I pounded my fist on his desk, and demanded, "I want to see Uncle Bing."

"Uncle Bing?" he asked, an amused grin tweaking his lips.

"My uncle," I corrected. "John Smith." I'd deepened my voice, letting him know that I meant business and wasn't about to keep up this silly cat-and-mouse game. "I want to see him *now!*"

The captain slid his chair back, making it screech as it slid across the floor that was in dire need of polish. "No problem. All you had to do was ask nicely." The grin he tossed my way made me want to reach out and strangle him, which was what I knew he wanted me to do so he could arrest me too. But I fluttered my eyes and grinned back.

"Thank you," I forced myself to say.

Clyde Bullhouser had been temporarily silenced by the captain's and my discussion. He obviously hadn't known I was a cop until now.

The three of us walked down the long hall, all the way to the back of the police station, where a double metal door greeted us. Now, the walls were gray. I shivered as I remembered the days when I had to do this very thing, only from the other side.

"Sign here," he ordered.

I jotted my name on the sign-in sheet; then Mr. Bullhouser did the same. It would have suited me just fine if he'd opted to stay in the lobby, but I couldn't keep him from going with me, since I'd already bullied him into driving me to the station.

Captain Stokes led us to a small room just on the other side of the security doors. "Be right back," he said as he backed out of the room.

Mr. Bullhouser and I didn't say a word to each other while we waited. I suspected he was still in a state of shock over the fact that I was a cop.

When I saw my uncle's face, I saw that Mr. Bullhouser wasn't the only person who was in a state of shock. I quickly stood and reached out for Uncle Bing.

Captain Stokes held me back. "You should know better than that," he said, leading my uncle over to the other side of the table. "No touching."

What did he think I'd do—slip Uncle Bing a metal file to break out of jail? Forcing myself to nod, I said, "Yes, I understand."

The captain backed out of the room and pointed to the window at the top of the door. "I'll be right out there, watching. So no funny stuff."

As soon as he was out of the room, Uncle Bing leaned across the table and said, "Why did you bring this joker along?"

"I needed a ride," I replied.

He sank back in his chair, a look of dejection and despair covering his face. "This is just awful," he finally said.

"Did you enjoy the ride over?" Clyde Bullhouser mocked.

"Why, you—" My uncle leapt from his chair and almost flew across the table when the door opened and

Captain Stokes glared at him. Uncle Bing sat back down.

I turned to the man next to me and ordered, "Stop it. I'm not here to listen to two grown men fighting like a couple of three year olds. If you can't control yourself, then leave now."

He held his hands up and shook his head. "I won't say a word," he said, smiling. Now that he'd gotten used to the fact that I knew what I was doing, he seemed to find humor in this situation. I wanted to deck him.

I spent the next ten minutes asking my uncle all sorts of procedural questions, making sure this small-town cop shop had covered all the bases. And they had. I had to give them credit for knowing proper procedures, but I was dismayed over the fact that I couldn't trip them up on technicalities. Now I understood how defense attorneys operated.

When my questions about his incarceration had dwindled and I'd begun to ask personal things, Uncle Bing hung his head and moaned, "I hate that you had to see all this, Summer. All my plans for your vacation, all my hopes to make you want to move to Gulfside . . ." His voice trailed off, and he looked away.

"Hey, Uncle Bing, don't worry," I said, holding my palms up to my side. "You didn't do anything wrong, other than be in the wrong place at the right time."

Bullhouser snorted a chuckle. I kicked him beneath the table. Uncle Bing shook his fist. "One more word out of you, Bullhouser, and they'll have a legitimate reason to keep me here."

"You can't handle rejection, can you, Bing?" Why didn't that man shut up before he got us all into trouble?

My uncle's face grew so red it was almost purple. I reached out and gripped Mr. Bullhouser's forearm. "I told you to stop it."

Bullhouser shrugged. "I was afraid Bing would come after me when he saw Bonita and me at the Nineteenth Hole last week. I had no idea he'd kill the old broad."

"Don't ever call her that again," Bing said through clenched teeth, his hands forming fists that looked like they might come across the table at any moment. If he gave in to his urge at the moment, he'd wind up being charged with two counts of murder.

These two men reminded me of the time when I'd witnessed a couple boys duke it out over a girl on the schoolyard back in junior high school. There definitely was a rivalry going on.

I darted a killer look to Uncle Bing, which seemed to hold him back for the time being. Only problem was, I didn't think he could keep his temper intact much longer.

Uncle Bing's frown deepened. "Has anyone told Alice about her mother?"

"Alice?" I asked, turning to Mr. Bullhouser.

He nodded. "Yeah, Bonita's daughter."

I shook my head. "I have no idea, but I can find out."

"I'll call her," Mr. Bullhouser said, looking at Uncle Bing without the anger I'd seen only a moment earlier.

"I'd certainly appreciate it, Clyde," Uncle Bing said. "Just make sure you tell her I didn't do it."

Mr. Bullhouser opened his mouth, then closed it when he looked at me. He obviously knew better than to keep provoking Uncle Bing, but I couldn't expect it to last.

"We'd better go now," I finally said.

The instant I said that, Captain Stokes was inside the room with us. If there was ever any doubt of whether we had privacy, it was gone now.

Okay, so now I had a better idea of what I was dealing with. My conviction of Uncle Bing's innocence was holding, and I could see that *President* Bullhouser most likely agreed with me. He enjoyed tossing barbs with Uncle Bing, but there was some strange sort of affection between these two guys.

Mr. Bullhouser and I watched as Uncle Bing was led away by the police captain. His head hung low, and he appeared to be emotionally beaten. My heart ached at the thought of what he was going through. And what hurt most was knowing that this was only the beginning.

During my twelve years with the Nashville Police Department, I probably only saw one or two innocent people charged with something as serious as murder. Normally, when we had someone in custody, we were almost one hundred percent certain they committed the crime. This was definitely an unusual case.

"What will you do now?" Mr. Bullhouser asked, as we got into his car.

I turned and glared at him. "What do you mean?"

He stuck the key in the ignition, turned it, and looked at me for a moment before he put the car in "drive." "Where will you go, now that the old guy is in the brig?"

Mr. Bullhouser enjoyed talking tough, most likely to get a rise out of me. But I wasn't taking the bait.

Tilting my head and raising one eyebrow, I replied, "I'm not going anywhere."

"You're not?" he asked nervously. "What kind of vacation is this? I thought you needed some R and R."

"I do, but now that this has happened, I think I need to stick around."

"If you wanna go off somewhere, I can look after things here," he offered.

I stared at him in disbelief. "You'd do that for me?" I asked.

"Sure, I would," he replied as he pulled up to a red light. Then, he looked me directly in the eye, and it dawned on him that I might not have been serious. "Wait a minute," he said. "You don't think I killed that old woman, do you?"

"The idea has occurred to me," I said, although I really didn't think he'd done it. He was too much of a clown—too showy.

He slammed his palm on the steering wheel. "That's the most ridiculous thing I've ever heard."

"So is the idea of Uncle Bing being the murderer."

"Well, I sure didn't do it."

"Whatever." I folded my arms over my chest and looked out the side window as we drove past tacky tourist beach shops. You've seen one beach town, you've seen 'em all.

After a few moments of silence, Mr. Bullhouser spoke up. "Ya know, Miss Walsh, I don't think I believe your story."

"You don't believe what story?"

"That you're a cop."

"What part about that don't you believe?" I asked.

"You're awfully small," he answered. "And pretty. Someone who looks like you doesn't have to get a job as a cop."

"Oh, really?" I said, now curious as to how he planned to stick his other foot in his mouth. "What kind of job can you see me doing?"

"Sales clerk in a ladies' boutique, maybe?" he said, throwing a self-satisfied grin my way. "Or hairdresser in some upscale, chic salon."

I couldn't think of anything else I'd rather *not* do. The thought of catering to another woman's vanity grated my nerves like nails on a chalkboard. "I've never done either of those things, and I doubt I ever will."

He shrugged. "You'd be good at it, I'm sure."

Now, I realized this joker actually meant this as a compliment. His impression of the ultimate job for a woman was working in a boutique.

"Thanks," I finally said, wanting nothing more than to be somewhere far away from this Casanova wannabe.

By the time we got to the condo building, everything was dark, with the exception of one street light that was illuminating the entire parking lot. "I'll walk you to your door," Mr. Bullhouser offered.

If nothing else, he was a gentleman.

I quickly sat up in bed as the ruckus from the parking lot below grew louder. Morning light sifted through the sheer curtains, illuminating the unfamiliar room. What in the—?

When I remembered where I was and what had happened last night, I flopped back onto my pillow. I was hoping it was all just one of those bad dreams where nothing made sense. But it was real. It still didn't make sense; I was actually living a nightmare.

I rubbed my eyes and sat up slowly this time. The noise downstairs was growing louder by the second. I stood up, crossed the room, and pulled back the blinds. There must have been a dozen elderly people, all talking at once, their voices rising to levels that would wake the dead.

There was no way I'd be able to get back to sleep, so I grabbed my suitcase, tossed it onto the bed, opened it, and pulled out the pair of cutoffs lying on top. I had a bunch of stuff to do anyway so I figured I might as well get started.

By the time I made it downstairs to the parking lot, there were only three people left—a woman with dyed black hair that must have held a whole can of hairspray, a bald guy, and Mr. Bullhouser. They all turned and glared at me when I appeared.

"What's going on?" I asked, trying hard to keep the annoyance from my voice.

The bald guy pointed to Mr. Bullhouser and said, "He started it."

"Started what?" I felt like a kindergarten teacher breaking up a fight on the playground. What was it people said about going through a second childhood?

"He said Bonita was a floozy," the man said. "I offered to rearrange his face, but Delta won't let me touch him."

Mr. Bullhouser chuckled. "Henry, you shouldn't let your ex-wife talk to you like that."

"But Delta—" the man Mr. Bullhouser had called Henry said, before he was interrupted.

Delta must have been the woman with the big hair. "Bonita was nothing but a loose woman, but she's dead now," she said in her thick Brooklyn accent. I noticed she wouldn't look me in the eye. "We shouldn't be saying bad things about the dead, even if she did get what was coming to her." She quickly looked down and added, "God rest her soul."

"Hold on," I said. "Wait a minute. Are you saying what I just thought you said?" Was I looking at the murderer right now? "Do you know something about Ms. Landry's murder?"

Henry's face contorted. "Maybe."

The woman cast a nervous scowl at Henry, who shrugged. When she turned back to me, she paused for a moment before she said, "Not really."

Okay, now we're getting somewhere, I thought. "Do you know who did it?" I asked Henry directly.

Delta swallowed hard and stepped in front of him, blocking him from my view. "It could be one of several people." She held her hands up and counted several people on her fingers. I noticed how her hands were shaking, but I let her talk. Then, she said a name I hadn't heard before now. "Tom Masterson, the tennis pro, is always complaining that Bonita never paid for her lessons on time. He always had to remind her."

"Aw, c'mon, Delta. That's not enough to pin a murder rap on anyone," Mr. Bullhouser said. I agreed with him. "He's a harmless nuisance, if you ask me."

Delta wagged her finger. "No one asked you."

I turned to her and smiled. It looked like it wouldn't take much to get her to talk. "What else do you know?"

"Well," she said in a shrill voice that cracked, "I do know that she was stepping out with Bing. She used to go to the clubhouse dances with Clyde, but he got fresh with her, so she told him to take a hike."

"Wait a minute," Mr. Bullhouser said, taking a step toward her. "I never did anything to her she didn't want me to do."

"No woman in her right mind would want your grubby mitts on her," the woman said, hands on her hips, making it obvious that she wasn't the least bit afraid of Clyde Bullhouser.

I knew that if I didn't do something quickly we'd have a fight on our hands, the way these two people's voices were elevating and their faces were turning red. "Hold on, you two," I said, taking a step between them. "We're not accomplishing a thing, standing out here arguing like this."

"I just don't like being accused of something I

didn't do," Mr. Bullhouser said, a pouty look crossing his face. He turned back to the woman and said, "Delta, get your facts straight before you go accusing people of things like that."

The woman they were calling Delta opened her mouth, but shut it quickly when I gave her my I'm-the-cop-in-control look. Man, it still worked, I thought with smug satisfaction. The saying "Once a cop, always a cop" rang through my head, making me wince and drop my temporary glee. I wanted to be a civilian, but now wasn't the time. I had to clear my uncle.

I instructed everyone to go back to their condos, telling them that I'd let them know when they were needed. My list of suspects was growing larger by the hour, and I imagined it would continue to swell before this whole thing was over. I let out a long sigh of frustration. My retirement from law enforcement seemed to be getting further and further from reach.

Chapter Four

Delta and the bald man left without any more argument, but Mr. Bullhouser seemed to enjoy annoying me. "What do we do now, Miss Walsh?"

I dropped my head forward a few inches, raised my eyebrows, and shot him a glance of disbelief. "We?"

He nodded and folded his arms over his chest. "Yeah, I wanna help. Maybe between the two of us, we can crack this case."

"Wait a minute," I said, shaking my head. "I thought you said my uncle was guilty."

"I'm not sure now. He looked pretty upset last night. Besides, I'm worried about you. Looks to me like you're bent on sticking your nose in all sorts of things around here, and I don't want you to get yourself in any trouble."

It took every ounce of self-restraint to keep from howling with laughter. "Trust me, Mr. Bullhouser. I'm fine. I've done this before."

"But—" he began.

I grinned at him as condescendingly as I was able to, stopping him in mid-sentence. "Don't worry about me. Just go about your everyday business and pretend I'm not here."

"I'm not sure if I can do that," he said slowly. "After all, I'm in charge here. This condo association is my responsibility, and I have to make sure you don't harass the kind people who live here."

"Trust me," I replied in my firm cop tone. "I won't harass anyone. That's not my style. Or are you worried I might discover something unsavory about you?"

"I don't think—" he began before Delta interrupted him.

"That's always been your problem," she said. "You never think." With a long-suffering sigh, she looked over her shoulder at her ex-husband and then back at me, but not directly. "If I didn't already have plans to leave for vacation this week, I'd help you get to the bottom of this."

"You never mentioned anything about vacation," Mr. Bullhouser said.

"I don't tell you everything I plan to do," she hissed back at him. She rolled her eyes and pulled at her earlobe. "I'm sure the police know what they're doing, so maybe we should all just leave well enough alone."

"Miss Walsh here used to be a cop," Mr. Bullhouser

blurted, almost as if he had bragging rights about my past.

"Don't try to interfere with the cops here in Gulfside," she said to me in warning, her face now drained of color. "They know this community better than anyone."

"I'll just visit with a few people and get to know some of Bonita Landry's friends," I said, nodding. The last thing I wanted to do was lessen a citizen's respect for the local law enforcement. "If I find out anything new I'll be sure to let the authorities handle it."

Mr. Bullhouser narrowed his gaze and glanced from Delta back to me. "You do that, Miss Walsh." He appeared to be playing out a scene from a television cop show.

Delta's ex-husband stepped out of the shadows and put in his two cents. "We don't need outsiders getting involved in our business."

As if it had been scripted, Mr. Bullhouser turned his head toward the building and then glanced at me out of the corner of his eye. "If I hear one thing about you being where you're not supposed to be, I'll personally see to it that you don't step foot in Condos on the Green, ever again."

Clyde Bullhouser was a man to reckon with, in his own mind. But I thought he was a humorous side-trip. He never ceased to sway with the wind, probably something he'd learned in condo politics. I made a mental note to run the other way if I saw him coming when I needed to get some serious work done. I had a feeling he was the type to circumvent all my efforts, making my investigation all the more difficult. Oh well, I'd dealt with this type of thing before, and I could certainly do it now. But still, Mr. Bullhouser was funnier than most.

It took me nearly an hour to write down all the names of the people I'd spoken with already. One person whose name I didn't have was the bald guy I assumed was Delta's ex-husband. I'd have to ask Mr. Bullhouser for that one.

He answered the door before I had a chance to make the second rap when I knocked. "So you changed your mind, Miss Walsh?"

I cleared my throat to keep from barking the thoughts that fled through my mind. "Uh, I do have a few quick questions."

"Come on in," he said as he held the door open for me. "I told you I'd give you a hand with this." He offered me a chair, but I just stood there and stared at him, so he backed off. "You know, Miss Walsh, I'm beginning to think Bing did it. After all, he was smitten with Bonita, and you know what they say about a jealous man."

No, I didn't know what they said about a jealous man, but I really didn't care. All I wanted was names. Besides, I knew Mr. Bullhouser didn't really think my uncle committed the crime. He was just trying to stir up more excitement.

"Look, Mr. Bullhouser, maybe I was wrong to brush you off like I did. You and I may disagree on whether or not my uncle committed the murder, but I'm sure that even *you* don't want him convicted if he's innocent." Using my best cop look, I leveled him with my gaze. He took a step back. "So I'll need your cooperation . . . and maybe a little assistance from you." Nothing wrong with giving him something to keep him busy and out of trouble, I figured.

Grinning from ear to ear, he nodded enthusiastically like a small child. "I'll do what I can to help."

Watching him acting so eager to help, I figured he was probably innocent. Either that or he was playing me for a complete and total fool, which I didn't think he was smart enough to do.

"Okay," I said as I finally took the chair he offered. I pulled my notepad from my purse and opened it to my list of contacts. "I need names."

"Names?" he parroted.

"Yes, names," I said. "Of people who knew the victim."

Mr. Bullhouser inhaled through his nose, making a snorting sound, and he quickly exhaled as he crossed the room to the breakfast bar between the kitchen and living room. "I can do you one better than that. I have the list of residents of Condos on the Green."

I had no idea it would be this easy. He was willing to just hand over a list of the residents in his association, when I was certain there was a rule against it somewhere in the condo documents. But who was I to argue?

With a smile, I gratefully accepted the list. Just as I was about to stick it in my purse, he reached out to grab it. "What do you think you're doing with that?"

I pulled it back out and held it barely out of his

reach. "Oh, is this not mine?" Of course, it wasn't. He just wanted me to look at it.

"I can't let you have that, Miss Walsh," he said in a tone that implied he thought I was an idiot. "If you need to write a few names down, I won't stop you, but I can't let you walk outa here with that list."

"Oh, okay," I said, pretending that I'd just caught on. Maybe it was in my best interest with this guy to play the stupid female. He obviously thought it anyway, so why not use it to help with my uncle's case?

It took me almost fifteen minutes to write the names and their condo numbers on my notepad. My writing was generally pretty sloppy, and I didn't want to take any chances of not being able to read it when I really needed it.

"Thanks, Mr. Bullhouser," I said as I stood up to leave. "I can't begin to tell you how much this helps."

"What's my next assignment?" he asked. I narrowed my eyes and took a good look at him. He was serious.

"Uh, why don't you see if you can find out who she spoke to yesterday?"

He nodded. "Will do. I saw her day before yesterday, and she said she was having coffee with Delta."

I'd started toward the door, but the instant he said Delta's name, I stopped in my tracks and turned to face him. "She did? What else did she say?"

Mr. Bullhouser shrugged, apparently pretty pleased with himself for being able to provide this information. "I dunno, just some stuff about getting back to the tennis court and taking another lesson."

Well, obviously, she'd been at the tennis court. After all, that was where her body was discovered. With Uncle Bing's handkerchief around her neck. That gave me the shivers. Not only had someone murdered this woman, they had the foresight to take something that belonged to him and use it against him later. It appeared to me that it was premeditated murder, but I still wasn't sure.

Armed with the names and the knowledge that I'd just bought some uninterrupted time, I left Mr. Bullhouser's condo. He assured me he'd have the information I needed by the time I returned.

Not wanting him to be the first to talk to the tennis pro, I went to the courts right away. One section of the court—the area closest to the pro shop—was still taped off. The tennis pro was giving a lesson on the other side, the furthest away from the building.

I went over and watched as he impatiently showed an elderly man the proper way to serve. I was not impressed. Who was he to say there was only one way to get the ball over the net? Personally, I found the man's style more appealing than the traditional way the pro was trying to show him.

Finally, the half hour was up, and it looked like the pro was free. I waited until the elderly gentleman had left the court before I made my move.

The tennis pro didn't look up, even though I made myself obvious by walking directly in front of his line of vision. He knew I was there, but he didn't say a word.

"You the tennis pro?" I asked. No answer. Maybe he was hard of hearing, but I doubted it. Still, I felt like I needed to speak a little louder to be sure. "I'm Summer Walsh, John Smith's niece." He looked at me like I'd just landed on a spaceship. "You know, John Smith. Bing."

A flicker of amusement flashed through his eyes. I hated the way his mustache twitched at the same time, but I forced myself to smile as I extended my hand.

He glanced down at my outstretched hand, but he didn't take it. He just went about his business picking up tennis balls.

"Look," I said as I followed him all over the court. "I'll only take a few minutes of your time. I wanted to talk to you about the woman who was murdered yesterday."

He finally stopped picking up tennis balls and turned to face me. "Look, Miss Walsh, I don't know what you're doing here or why you feel like you need to bother me right now. I've spoken to my attorney, and he told me to keep my mouth shut unless he's present."

"Your attorney?" I asked. Now we were getting somewhere. This man, this tennis pro, had felt it necessary to hire an attorney. But why? As far as I knew, he wasn't a suspect. The only suspect the cops had was in custody.

The man nodded as if he felt he might have already said too much. "If you want information, talk to the cops. I told them everything I know."

"Oh, you did, did you?" I asked. "Did you remember to tell them about how Miss Landry never paid for her lessons on time?"

His face turned bright red with fury. "Who told you that?"

Squaring my shoulders, knowing that I'd finally gotten to him, I smiled and took my time answering. Then, slowly I replied, "It's common knowledge that Ms. Landry didn't feel the need to pay her bills until she got her money's worth. And from the way you handled that last gentleman, I'd say I couldn't blame her."

His face grew so red, I thought he'd blow a gasket. Good. That was exactly the reaction I wanted. His temper was hot, and his fuse was short. It wouldn't take much to get him excited.

"Well, I can see I'm not welcome around here, Mr. Masterson. I'll tell the cops what I know, and I'm sure they'll want to discuss it with you." I allowed a few seconds to lapse before I added, "And I have no doubt they'll like to hear how mad you were that I stopped by to chat with you. I have a feeling Ms. Landry didn't feel it necessary to pay for your temper tantrums."

The hardest thing I had to do at that moment was turn my back and start walking away. It was risky. He'd either let me go, or he'd call me back, the very thing I wanted him to do. If he called me back, I knew it would be to talk.

I was all the way to the parking lot before I heard his strained voice. "Miss Walsh!"

Yes! It took every ounce of self-restraint to turn around slowly. I wanted to jump back and shake the information out of him. But I couldn't. I had to act like it was a pain to have to turn around and go back.

"What, Mr. Masterson?" I asked, with the most exasperated tone I could fake. "Did you forget something?"

He held a tennis racket in one hand as he stood there, trying to decide what he should say, or if he should say anything. I didn't want to give him time to think, so I turned back around and started to leave again.

"Wait!" he commanded.

"What?" I called over my shoulder as I kept walking. "I don't have all day."

"If you have about ten minutes, I can tell you a few things, but you can't use any of it against me. I didn't do it."

I had to smile. This man was even more stupid than I'd originally thought. Glancing at my watch, I spun around and faced him. "Five minutes. I've got things to do."

He told me more in that five minutes than I'd ever managed to get in a formal interview with a suspect. And by the time I left, I knew there were more possibilities than I'd ever imagined. It seemed that this Bonita Landry was the most disliked woman in all of Gulfside. Not only did she play one man against another, she didn't even care if they were married. And she took advantage of people like Tom Masterson, who extended credit on services, such as tennis lessons and other interests she had.

"If I wanted to kill her, I never would have left her lying face down right in the middle of the tennis court.

It's too obvious," he said with a nervous crack in his voice.

"Oh?" I asked. "What would you have done with the body?"

With a slight shrug, he replied, "I don't know. Maybe I would have dumped her in the woods back there." He pointed to a heavily forested section of the swamp that had been cleared for this development.

Nodding, I said, "I see. It would have been much more difficult to trace back to you if she was in there."

He chuckled a little too heartily. "You know what I mean."

"Yes," I replied. "I do know exactly what you mean."

As I left the tennis pro standing there with his mouth hanging open, wondering what happened just now, I thought about how I'd made him squirm. It was tempting to put him out of his misery and tell him I didn't consider him a suspect, but I wanted to keep him guessing, just in case I needed more information on anyone else added to the suspect list.

Chapter Five

"No, Miss Walsh," Captain Stokes said. "Your uncle isn't eating much." He stood up and came around from behind his huge metal desk. I would have thought they'd have something a little nicer for the head of the department, even in Gulfside. "Why?"

With a slight shrug of one shoulder, I glanced down at the paperwork he had strewn on his desk. There were piles of traffic tickets, all of them going approximately the same speed. I took a step closer to see the location. Yep. Just as I'd thought. Gulfside had a speed trap. Probably their number two source of income, right behind property taxes.

"I'm worried about him," I replied. "He's always been a picky eater." Then, I started in on what I'd come there for. "I spoke to Tom Masterson."

"Tennis pro?" he asked quickly, letting me know he'd already spoken with the man.

I nodded. "He's a real piece of work, that man. I have a feeling he's frustrated."

"What are you getting at?" Captain Stokes asked.

Tilting my head to one side, grazing the room with my gaze, I snickered. "I'm not so sure you've investigated this case as thoroughly as you could. There are other people out there who had a motive to kill Bonita Landry. I got a list of names a mile long from Mr. Masterson."

Captain Stokes's face grew bright crimson. "You seem to forget, Miss Walsh, that we have evidence. That handkerchief even had your uncle's monogram, and he admitted that it was his."

"That's not evidence, Captain Stokes," I retorted, leaning toward him with my knuckles resting on the edge of his desk. "You know as well as I do that people plant evidence all the time. Don't tell me you're taking the easy way . . . no, the lazy way out."

I thought he was going to explode right then and there. I'd insulted this police officer to make my point, and he was ready to fight.

"Get out of my office, Miss Walsh," he said, pointing to the door. "And if you keep antagonizing the good citizens of Gulfside, I'll have to force you to leave town."

I raised my eyebrows and shot him a glance that let him know I knew my rights. "I'm surprised at you, Captain Stokes. I would have thought you'd know better than to do this to a guest of your fine town. What kind of public relations is that? I might have to call the motor club and let them know how you treat tourists."

The color drained from his face. My silly little threat had unhinged him. Obviously, the motor club meant something to him. I did know that tourism was a big industry for them; in fact, all the charter fishing boats and restaurants depended on vacationers to stay in business.

After he had a moment to calm down, he cleared his throat. "Okay, Miss Walsh, tell you what. You can stay in Gulfside, but don't talk to so many people."

"I can't make that promise," I said. "You know that. My uncle's in jail for a crime he didn't commit."

Captain Stokes chewed the inside of his lip as he thought for a moment. I could tell I had him stumped. He'd never had to back down before, and he didn't quite know how to do it without losing face.

"Tell you what," I finally said. "I'll chat with some of Uncle Bing's neighbors, and if I hear anything of any value in this case, I'll bring the information to you."

He paused for a few seconds, then nodded. "Just don't make a pest of yourself, and whatever you do, don't make anyone think we're suspicious of them. People here don't take kindly to accusations and threats."

I gasped in mock horror. "I'd never threaten anyone, Captain Stokes."

His confused expression almost had me laughing out loud. He'd considered my very existence a threat, not to mention my plan to talk to the motor club about how unwelcome guests were in this town. At least I knew how to handle Captain Stokes. Maybe he'd eventually come around if I played my cards right.

Just as I was about to leave his office, he called my name. "Uh, Miss Walsh?"

I spun around and faced him, forcing a smile as pleasant as I could manage. "Yes?"

"Would you like to have dinner with me tonight?" he asked, his fingertips nervously drumming on the side of his desk.

My first impulse was to glance down at his left ring finger. Heck, I'd always done that. Even cops cheated on their wives, and I wasn't into that sort of thing.

His finger was ringless, no sign of a wedding band tan. Captain Stokes wasn't exactly my type, but I didn't want to antagonize the poor man. Slowly nodding, I replied, "Sounds good. I'll meet you somewhere."

He opened his mouth to argue, but he snapped it shut and nodded. I waited for a moment for him to tell me where we'd meet. When he didn't, I finally had to ask. "When and where would you like to have dinner?"

After another long pause, he frowned and said, "We can just meet here. I'll let you talk with your uncle first, then we can go somewhere on the beach."

I hadn't thought much about food since my uncle had been jailed. Suddenly, my stomach growled, reminding me that I hadn't eaten since last night. "Okay," I said. "What time?"

"Five okay?" he asked.

That was awful early, but I had to remember that this was a small town, and most of the population probably went to bed early. I nodded. "Five sounds good. How long you gonna let me talk to Uncle Bing?"

"As long as you want," he replied, appearing to feel pretty good about things, and I assumed, generous. "Just don't do anything funny that will get me into trouble."

He was so transparent. He wanted to keep me happy so I wouldn't make him the laughingstock of Gulfside, or Florida for that matter. When the town had to pick their law enforcement leaders, they probably didn't have much to choose from. In fact, they were pretty lucky to have someone like Captain Stokes, who seemed to know the rules. In my previous experience, some small town cops didn't have a clue as to what proper police procedures were. But then, they generally didn't need to since most of them rarely had to deal with serious crime.

When I left his office, I felt like someone had beaten me with a stick. Captain Stokes had a way of making me feel like I was under a magnifying glass when I was in the same room with him, almost as if he thought I might have been involved in the murder somehow, which was ridiculous since I wasn't even in town when it allegedly happened.

I made it back to Uncle Bing's condo and flopped over on the bed. The noise that had awakened me that morning was long gone. After squinting for several minutes, I stood up, crossed the room, and shut the blinds to block the sunlight that wouldn't let up. Another reason not to consider moving to Florida.

I tried to nap for a couple of hours before I began to hear cars in the parking lot. No wonder Uncle Bing made this his guest bedroom, I thought. His was in the back of the condo, facing the natural preserve. Maybe I should consider staying in his room, I thought, at least until we could get him out of jail.

I've never been able to nap in the middle of the day, especially at someone else's place, and this was no exception. A couple of times I drifted off to sleep, but some unfamiliar sound woke me. After the second time this happened, I decided to give up trying to get some rest. Besides, I had work to do. Clearing Uncle Bing wouldn't be easy.

My list had a bunch of names and condo numbers. The only people I knew anything about were the ones who'd spoken directly to me, and they were all suspects in my eyes. At least, it seemed that they all had a reason to dislike Bonita Landry, even though I didn't see a single reason to kill her. But I had to remember that most people didn't kill others. It took something, often something indefinable, to push someone over the edge. I just had to find out who disliked her the most and see if I could find evidence on that person. However, I was also aware of the fact that dislike wasn't the only motive for killing. Perhaps her daughter would know something. In fact, that seemed the logical place to start.

Mr. Bullhouser didn't answer his door when I

knocked, but I saw that his car was in the parking lot. Either he didn't hear me, or he was avoiding me. I went back to Uncle Bing's condo and tried calling. He answered on the second ring.

"This is Summer Walsh. I need to talk to you for a few minutes," I said as soon as he said hello.

He let out a deep breath of exasperation. Had he grown tired of playing cop already? "I've already told you everything I know. I was hoping you'd leave me alone by now."

"You know I can't do that as long as my uncle's still in jail."

"He could be in there for a very long time, Miss Walsh. Surely, you don't plan to stay in his place for the next twenty years to life."

I managed a short chuckle. My uncle was in his seventies. I doubted he'd be in jail twenty years, even if he *was* found guilty.

"Okay, what more do you want from me?" he finally asked.

"I need to know how to get ahold of Ms. Landry's daughter."

"Why should I tell you?"

"Somehow, I thought you'd want to," I said. I was growing even more impatient now, and I didn't feel like playing these stupid games. "Don't you want to find out who killed Ms. Landry?"

"Well, yes, but I don't want you bothering Alice. Bonita and her daughter didn't exactly get along. In fact, I don't think they've spoken in nearly a year."

Aha! So we were getting somewhere. "Her own

daughter doesn't speak to her?" I asked. "Any idea why?"

"I dunno." Mr. Bullhouser probably knew he'd already said too much. "Probably has something to do with money."

"Cops know?" I asked.

"How should I know?" he asked defensively.

There he goes again, I thought. "Because I figured you might have told them."

"Well, maybe I mentioned it."

He sure wasn't cooperating like I thought he should. If this man didn't open up and give me the information I wanted, I decided, I was going to resort to fear tactics. I wasn't one who liked others wasting my time.

"Look, Mr. Bullhouser," I said in my best cop voice. "I'm beginning to think you were somehow involved." That wasn't exactly the truth, but I needed to get his attention again, since I seemed to have lost it.

"You're just beginning to think that?" he asked with a snort. "I think you've had your sights on me since this whole thing started."

"Maybe I have," I quipped. "And if you don't come forth with everything you know, I'll have to start looking into your background."

"You can't do that," he said in a voice that had suddenly turned shaky.

"I can and will do whatever it takes to find out who killed Ms. Landry. The only thing I know for certain is that my uncle didn't do it. Now are you gonna cooperate or not?"

All I had to do now was play the waiting game. Mr.

Bullhouser could take all day if he wanted, but I wasn't going to make a sound until he did.

"Oh, all right, Miss Walsh. Bonita has grandchildren you can talk to. I don't know anything about her grandson. He's sort of the artistic type, and he roams around the country in his van. Let me see if I can find her granddaughter's phone number."

"She has a granddaughter?"

"Yes, her name's Tiffany."

"Does Tiffany ever come around?"

Mr. Bullhouser shrugged. "When she can. She lives in Mississippi."

"Mississippi?" I asked. "Ms. Landry was from Mississippi?"

"No," he replied. "Her granddaughter's husband, Shark, is stationed at the air force base on the Mississippi Gulf Coast. Bonita is from Ohio."

For someone who wasn't romantically involved with Bonita Landry, Clyde Bullhouser sure did know a lot about her. "Any idea where her daughter lives?" I asked.

"Why, she lives in Gulfside," he said.

Chapter Six

She lives in Gulfside? Have I seen her? I wondered. "Where?" I asked. I did my best to cover up my shock that she was so close yet I hadn't seen her.

He chuckled. "Now that I don't know."

"Do you have an address?"

"I'm sure you can find out from the local authorities," he said. "After all, they know something about everyone in this town."

I was ready to scream. Mr. Bullhouser sure could be bullheaded when he took a mind to.

Since I could tell I was getting nowhere fast with this guy, I got off the phone with him as quickly as I could. I'd have to go about this a little differently. Maybe he was right; maybe Captain Stokes would know something.

I was ready and waiting at the police station when Captain Stokes arrived. He was wearing a royal blue polo shirt and khaki slacks, and I have to admit, he didn't look half bad. In fact, if we'd met under different circumstances, I might have actually enjoyed looking at the man. But as it was, I was only doing this for business—Uncle Bing's business.

"You're early," he said, as a crooked grin formed on his lips.

I narrowed my eyes. "You would be too, if your uncle was sitting in jail for something he didn't do."

"Maybe so," he said as he unlocked the door to his office. He opened his desk drawer and pulled out a set of keys. "Come on."

I followed him down the hall, to the small jail they had in the back of the building. This place definitely was *not* maximum security. In fact, I was surprised that they kept murder suspects here so long without any concern about a break.

Uncle Bing's face lit up when he saw me. "Summer! What are you still doing here? I would have thought you'd have left by now."

"No way, Uncle Bing," I said, forcing myself to smile back at him. For the first time, I noticed how deep the lines were around his eyes and forehead. He looked like he'd aged ten years since yesterday. My heart twisted.

As soon as Captain Stokes left my uncle and me alone in the interrogation/visiting room, I began asking the questions I'd formulated that day. "Tell me everything you know about Bonita Landry," I started.

Uncle Bing leaned forward and let his breath out in a whoosh. "She was one fine woman."

It was obvious that he really liked the woman, but that wasn't what I was talking about. "I'm sure she was, but I want to know some facts about her. I understand her daughter lives in Gulfside."

He nodded. "Yes, she does."

"Did they ever see each other?" I asked, prodding my uncle to tell me more.

"Not as much as Bonita would have liked. Her daughter isn't the friendliest person I know."

"You know her?" I asked.

"Yes, unfortunately, Bonita and I ran into her a few times when we went out."

"What's her daughter's name?"

"Alice," he replied. "Alice Hunt."

"Is she married?"

He nodded. "For the fourth time. In fact, last time I saw her was when she invited her mother to the wedding."

"But I thought they were estranged," I said. This whole thing wasn't making a bit of sense to me.

"I thought so too, but according to Bonita, Alice told her that the man she was about to marry wanted the whole family present."

"Any idea why?" I asked.

"Alice said that family was important to Barney. He didn't like the idea of Alice not speaking to Bonita."

I leaned back and thought about that. "So things got better between Ms. Landry and her daughter?"

"Not exactly," he replied. "Bonita tried her best to

be close to both Alice and Barney, but once the wedding was over, they tried to shut her out again."

"But I thought Barney was family oriented."

"So did Bonita, but she quickly discovered otherwise."

"Did he do something?" I glanced at my watch and saw that I'd been with Uncle Bing for nearly fifteen minutes, and all I had from him was a little family gossip about the murdered woman. I needed more.

Uncle Bing shrugged. "He didn't exactly do anything, except look at Bonita's bank books. The man's an investments counselor, and he offered to help her with her investments."

The skin on my spine tingled, just like it always had when I got close to valuable information on a case. "Investments? Did she have money?"

He chuckled. "Not really. She had enough to pay cash for her condo, with a little left to supplement her social security."

"I bet Barney was disappointed," I said.

Nodding, Uncle Bing agreed. "That's an understatement. His disappointment quickly turned to anger toward Alice."

"Anger?" Now we were getting somewhere.

"Yeah." Uncle Bing rubbed his chin. "Last time Bonita and I went out, she told me that Alice and Barney told her they never wanted to see her again and that she was to stay away from their house on the beach."

"They live on the beach?" Property there was premium, and the prices were sky high. Barney must have done quite well to have been able to afford a house on the beach.

Uncle Bing nodded again. "His last wife died and left him her family inheritance. He had to fight her kids for it, but he wound up with the lion's share of the money and the house."

Sounded to me like we were onto something. "I wonder why they didn't keep fighting," I said softly as my thoughts began to swirl with all kinds of possibilities of what could have happened to Bonita Landry. I had a gut feeling that I was so close to finding out what happened, but I couldn't for the life of me figure out exactly what it was.

He inhaled and exhaled, his forehead crinkling as if deep in thought. Then, his eyebrows dropped, hooding his eyes. "Seems to me they did try to fight it, but something happened, and they ran scared."

"Something happened?" I asked, my instincts kicking into high gear.

Uncle Bing nodded. "Yes, but I don't recall exactly what it was."

"But I thought Barney was family oriented," I said.

"He made noises like he was. When he was looking over Bonita's bank books, he seemed happy as a clam."

"Tell me exactly what changed things. He found out she didn't have money?"

"That's what I thought, but based on what Bonita told me, Barney thought she still had money."

"Okay, Uncle Bing," I said, my confusion even

worse. "Please explain. I need to know so I can help you."

Uncle Bing held his hands out, palms up as he spoke. This was a sign that he was being open and honest with me. "Bonita was worried that her daughter and son-in-law would think less of her if they knew how little she had. So she added a zero to the fifty grand, making them think she was worth half a million."

"Why did she care?" I asked.

"Apparently, Alice told her that it was important to Barney that she came from a good family, and in Alice's book, that meant a lot of money."

"That's the most ridiculous thing I've ever heard. Money has nothing to do with the quality of a family."

Uncle Bing smiled. "My sister taught you well."

I had to get back to the subject. "So as he went over her books, he saw the five hundred thousand. What did Ms. Landry want him to do?"

Uncle Bing shrugged. "He recommended several investments, but she told him she wasn't interested."

"And that's when they had the argument?" I asked.

"Well, not exactly. He continued being nice—I think that's what young people call sucking up—to stay in her good graces. I told Bonita that she needed to come clean and tell him she'd only added the zeros to impress him."

"And she did that?"

"Yes," he replied. "But she'd waited long enough so that he didn't believe her when she told the truth. In fact, I believe this is when the big rift began, but I wouldn't bet my life on it. He told her she was a liar and a cheap one at that."

Man, we were so close. I just knew it! "Please think about it, Uncle Bing. We might need this information to get you released."

"I don't see how that has anything to do with Bonita's death. After all, she was on the tennis court when they found her."

"Yes," I agreed, "and wearing your handkerchief around her neck. Any idea how it got there?"

"I gave it to her last weekend," he replied. "We went to the dollar movie where they play old shows. She started crying and sniffling during a sad scene— you know, how women do—and I handed her my handkerchief. When she was finished with it, she stuck it in her purse."

"Did you tell the cops who arrested you?" I asked.

Uncle Bing made a sour face. "I tried, but they told me they had witnesses to her murder."

"Witnesses?" I shrieked.

The door opened, and Captain Stokes peeked inside. "You okay, Miss Walsh?"

Nodding, I waved him away. As soon as the door was closed, I turned back to Uncle Bing. I forced my voice to come out in a whisper so the captain wouldn't hear me. "No one told me there were witnesses. Who?"

Uncle Bing shrugged. "Darned if I know. The only person who talked to the cops after we got there was Delta. They won't let me anywhere near these people. But I do know one thing. They're lying."

"That goes without saying," I agreed. "Because if there were witnesses to her death, they'd know that you had nothing to do with it."

"That's for sure," he said. "Wanna know who I think killed her?"

Leaning forward again, I nodded. "You have some ideas?"

Nodding, Uncle Bing replied, "I think it was the tennis pro."

"I thought about that, but I can't find a strong enough motive."

He smirked. "Bonita didn't like the squirrelly little guy, and he's a lousy tennis coach. So she often refused to pay him."

"He wouldn't kill someone for that," I said.

With another shrug, Uncle Bing said, "Maybe not, but I can't imagine who would be low-down enough to do something like kill her."

"Do you know something about the tennis pro I need to know?"

"Not really," he said.

With conviction that I was right, I said, "The tennis pro didn't do it. I'm pretty sure of that."

"Yeah," Uncle Bing said, his face showing frustration. "You're probably right. But I know he really needs the money. His mother is threatening to cut him off."

"His mother?" Ted Masterson must have been forty if he was a day.

"She's been supporting him ever since he quit his corporate job. I've heard he's the only one in his family who's not a millionaire in his own right. His brother-in-law is the CEO of the corporation that owns the country club." Uncle Bing was drumming his fingers on the table, and he'd begun to look around the room. I suspected this whole incarceration thing was starting to get to him.

"No one has secrets around here, do they?" I finally asked. Another reason not to live in Gulfside. Not that I had any secrets, but I sure didn't want everyone knowing my personal business.

"No, and that's the beauty of the place. Everyone knows everyone else." Bing actually still looked proud to be a resident of this place, even though he was a prisoner.

The door opened again, and Captain Stokes stuck his head inside. "Wrapping it up anytime soon?"

I started to shake my head no, but Uncle Bing stood up. "Yeah, I'm ready to call it a day. I'm getting pretty tired."

"Okay, let's get you back to your cell, Mr. Smith," Captain Stokes said in a gruff voice that I suspected was reserved for people in custody.

Uncle Bing walked a half step ahead of the police captain, while I waited in the room. There was so much information that just didn't make sense, I suspected I'd have to write everything down and look for some connecting threads. Most of the time, once everyone gave their stories, some common denominator could be found. Until then, I knew I'd be confused.

"How'd it go?" Captain Stokes said when he came back to get me.

"How'd what go?" I asked, stalling for time before blasting him with questions.

He narrowed his eyes and pursed his lips. I was annoying him, which didn't surprise me. I had that effect on plenty of people when I didn't get what I wanted.

Finally, he answered, "The visit."

"The visit," I repeated, still holding off telling him my thoughts. Should I or shouldn't I? I decided to jump in and start asking a few questions of my own. "How many other suspects do you have in this case?"

Captain Stokes looked at me as if he thought I'd lost my mind. "Look, Miss Walsh, I know you don't think your uncle did it, but we have proof."

"Proof?" I asked, glaring at him again.

"Yeah, proof," he said, glancing away, not daring to hold my gaze. I suspected I made him very uncomfortable with my knowledge of police procedures. Good.

"Okay, aside from a monogrammed hanky and some people who say they witnessed the crime, what proof do you have?" I shut my mouth to let him answer.

"That's all the proof we need in order to hold him." Captain Stokes sucked in a breath as his face turned bright red. Finally, when he expelled the breath, he said, "There are other things I haven't told you about."

"Like what?" I asked.

"Some things your uncle has done in the past that have caused us to keep a close eye on him."

"My uncle was under surveillance?" I shrieked. "Uncle Bing is a very friendly man, sometimes maybe even too friendly. I'll even admit that he's quite a flirt when it comes to the ladies, but he's actually pretty harmless. I've known him all my life, and I've never seen him hurt a single person."

"Then he didn't tell you about the time he hit Clyde Bullhouser, did he?"

"He hit him?" Uncle Bing couldn't possibly have done that. He didn't fight. "Surely, you're mistaken."

"No," Captain Stokes replied. "When Delta called and filed a complaint on his behalf, your uncle didn't deny striking him. He even bragged about how he was fighting for a woman's honor."

"Maybe you can tell me exactly what happened, then," I said. "Fighting for a woman's honor doesn't exactly make a man dangerous."

"It does if he sends the victim to the hospital. Mr. Bullhouser had to get stitches, and he came out with a black eye."

I had to force myself to keep from smiling. Somehow, I had the feeling Mr. Bullhouser deserved a black eye. "Who was the woman?"

"Who do you think?" Captain Stokes asked.

"Ms. Landry?"

He nodded. "And that's not all. Your uncle was seen climbing out of the window of another condo a month later. His fingerprints were all over the place."

"Did you arrest him then?" I asked, totally stunned

to hear all this about the uncle I'd always considered harmless. Maybe there was more to Uncle Bing than I realized.

"No," he replied. "When Delta got finished with old Henry, the poor guy didn't know whether he was coming or going."

"Delta? You mean the woman with the big black hair?" I asked. This Delta woman's name kept popping up. Henry must have been her bald little ex-husband.

"That's the one," he replied. "Henry spotted John Smith crawling out of the front window of her condo, so he went to Clyde Bullhouser's place to call us. We told him not to go inside until we got there, but he didn't listen. By the time we arrived, Delta was giving him a tongue-lashing like you've never seen, telling him that it was his fault she had to call John Smith. Seems she heard a noise, and she was scared, since it was one o'clock in the morning."

"But why was Uncle Bing climbing out of her window?" I asked. None of this was making a bit of sense to me. The more information I got, the more confused I became.

"She saw her ex-husband coming home. He lives in the condo right above her, you know. And she knew he'd jump to conclusions, so she told your uncle to leave from the window rather than have to face a confrontation."

Now I had to ask the next logical question. "What was Henry doing out at one o'clock in the morning?"

Captain Stokes grinned. "This is where it really gets

good. Seems Bonita Landry and Henry had something going on. At least, that's what people were saying at the time. Problem was, Henry wasn't enough of a man for her, and she told him so."

I shook my head. It was hard for me to imagine something like this happening among the senior set, but then I remembered something an old sergeant once told me. "People never really change that much. They just get even more like themselves as they get older. A grouch will get grouchier, and a sweet young woman will bake cookies for all the neighborhood children when she gets old." Looked to me like Bonita Landry might have been quite a femme fatale, and it backfired.

"Seems to me like you might have had more than one suspect," I said. "Arresting my uncle on the day of the murder was jumping the gun, in my opinion."

He shook his head. "We have to look at all the evidence. All arrows point to him. Besides we had to do something to keep the confidence of the citizens."

Obviously, Captain Stokes wasn't budging on this issue. It annoyed me, but I understood where he was coming from. To someone who didn't know Uncle Bing, he did look awfully guilty. And he never once denied having seen her and the fact that she enjoyed making men jealous.

Captain Stokes asked me to call him Jerry, which was difficult for me, since he looked more like a Bob or Bill, not to mention the fact that it galled me to be on first name terms with the man who held the key to my uncle's jail cell. But I knew it was in Uncle Bing's and my best interest to be nice to the man.

Jerry took me to the Barefoot Bar and Grille, a cozy little place overlooking the beach. It was built on stilts, and we had to walk up some wooden steps to get to the main dining room, where waitresses and bartenders wore yellow t-shirts with a huge black footprint emblazoned on the front. They were going for atmosphere.

I ordered a grouper sandwich, and Jerry got a double burger with cheese. Considering the fact that they specialized in seafood, I thought it was strange, but everyone has different taste, so I didn't make my customary sarcastic comments.

We were chatting about the afternoon showers they were expecting in Gulfside, when his eyes widened. "Don't look now, but here comes a couple of Gulfside's most prominent residents."

Naturally, I ignored his request and turned around to see who'd just walked in the door. "Who's that?"

He groaned. "I told you not to look. You might be interested in knowing that the woman is Alice Hunt, daughter of the deceased."

"They don't look all that grief-stricken to me," I said. "If my mother had been found murdered the day before, my eyes would look like road maps."

"I know what you mean," he said. Leaning even closer, he whispered, "If you want my honest opinion, I don't think she's all that upset about her mom being murdered."

Both the woman and the man who'd just walked in

had smiles plastered across their faces. And they were loud. Obviously, they were regular customers at the Barefoot Bar and Grille. Everyone in the place knew them.

"Jerry!" the man's voice boomed from about ten feet behind me. I cringed. They'd spotted us.

Captain Stokes . . . I mean Jerry offered a closed-mouth smile and a raised hand. "Barney," he said with a nod. "Alice."

They made their way to our table and stood over us as if they were inspecting meat in a deli counter. "Who's this?" Barney asked flirtatiously.

Jerry's eyes darted back and forth between Barney and me. I nodded my permission to introduce me.

"Uh, this is Summer Walsh," he said. "Barney and Alice Hunt."

Alice squinted and smiled with tight lips. "Do I know you?" she asked. "Your name sounds awfully familiar."

I felt Jerry's shoe nudge my leg beneath the table, which I took as a signal that he didn't want me to say I was the niece of her mother's alleged murderer. But I ignored him.

"Oh, Alice," I said as sympathetically as I could. "I'm so sorry to hear about what happened to your mother. You must be feeling awful."

Alice's expression suddenly changed. She looked totally baffled. "Did you know my mom?"

I shook my head and saw Jerry's horrified expression out of the corner of my eye. But I continued to ignore his warning. "I wish I had. From what I hear, she was quite a woman."

Barney snorted. "Yeah, old Bonita was quite a woman, all right."

Alice nudged him in the ribs. Openly. He didn't even try to hide his contempt for the victim of the tragedy only a day ago.

Going for full shock, I continued. "My uncle is totally distraught over this whole thing. If he weren't in jail, he'd be out looking for the person who did it."

Alice's eyebrows came together in a tight pinched look. "Your uncle's in jail? Whatever for?"

"The murd—" I began before I felt the toe of Jerry's shoe jabbing me in the shin. I just clamped my mouth shut and grinned.

"How's the fishing, Barney?" Jerry asked. "I heard the tarpon are running this week."

Still frowning, Barney turned and looked at the police captain. "I don't go for tarpon. I'm strictly into the small fish."

Alice's attention had been pulled away from our table by a group of casually dressed but over-jeweled people on the other side of the room. "Oh, look, there's Buffy and the clan."

Barney glanced up and nodded, pulling Alice over toward their friends. "See ya, Jerry." Then, he looked at me through squinted eyes and left.

"Strange people," I said as soon as they were out of earshot.

"What were you trying to do just now?" Jerry growled.

"I have no idea what you mean." Taking a sip of my lemonade, I tried my best to play dumb.

"You almost ruined my investigation."

"Your investigation?" I asked. "Of what?"

"Bonita Landry's death," he said in a whisper.

"But I thought—"

He interrupted me. "I know what you thought. We had to arrest your uncle, but I don't think for a minute that he did it. I wasn't gonna tell you this, but I had him locked up to get him out of the way. Besides, I figured people would be a little more open if they thought we didn't have any more suspects."

Aha! I had him on a technicality. He couldn't imprison my uncle if he didn't actually consider him a suspect. I started to tell him he'd better release my uncle, but he kept talking.

"I just hope you don't go and do something stupid, like try to turn this thing around and get him released. As it is, we're getting more information from people than we ever imagined we would."

"You are?"

"Yeah, people love to spill what they know about not only Bonita Landry, but your uncle. In fact, I have a sneaking suspicion that he might have been next on their hit list."

Chapter Seven

Oh, wow. Jerry actually thought my uncle's life might be in danger! Maybe I needed to find out exactly what Captain Jerry Stokes had up his sleeve before I jumped into springing Uncle Bing.

Over the next two hours, Jerry told me his plans for the investigation. "And I don't mind if you get involved as long as you keep me abreast of everything you're doing. I don't want to risk losing what we have on this case."

I nodded my assent. Maybe I'd cooperate . . . a little. But I still had some things I wanted to look into. Especially now that I'd met Alice and Barney.

"Have you checked them out?" I asked, tilting my head toward Ms. Landry's daughter and son-in-law.

"We're working on it," he admitted. "But so far

we're coming up with nothing. It's not like the woman had any money they'd be interested in."

I told him what I knew about Barney looking over Bonita's bank books. He nodded. "Yes, I'm aware of that. He still thinks there's money, but your uncle is on all Bonita Landry's accounts."

"My uncle is? Why?"

Jerry shrugged. "Apparently, Ms. Landry figured that since she was getting up there in age, she needed to do something to protect her assets. She put John . . . er, Bing's name on the accounts."

"But there's not that much money."

"I know that, and you know that, but try convincing someone like him," he replied, discreetly pointing to Alice and Barney in the midst of their showy friends.

"Does it have to be about money?" I asked, now fascinated by how things had turned around. Before now, I'd thought of Jerry as a fool for sticking my uncle in jail. I still didn't like what he was doing, but at least he thought he was protecting Uncle Bing.

He shrugged. "There might have been a different motive, but I don't know for sure yet."

"You're saying you think Alice and Barney had something to do with it?" So far, they were the only ones who might have benefited financially from Bonita Landry's death, at least from what I could tell.

Jerry shrugged. "Looks that way to me, but I could be wrong. That's why we're doing things this way. The chief didn't want to hold your uncle, but I convinced him to do it."

Swallowing hard, I nodded. "I don't like my uncle

being locked up, but I have to trust you on this." I swallowed hard and leaned toward him. "I want your word that as soon as you have enough evidence on someone else, you'll let him go."

He held up his hands. "Hey, I'm not saying your uncle is innocent. In fact, he's still the person we have the most evidence on at the moment."

I looked at him, studying his facial expressions for a long time. He really didn't think Uncle Bing killed Ms. Landry—that much was obvious now. Why I hadn't seen that in him before, I don't know, but I could tell he thought my uncle was innocent, and was not just blowing smoke.

"He told me he gave Ms. Landry the handkerchief during a sad movie." That handkerchief was the only evidence I knew about.

"I suspected it was something like that. The two of them were an item, although I heard your uncle wasn't interested in taking the relationship to the altar, which was precisely where Ms. Landry wanted it to go."

"Really?" I asked, my voice squeaking in surprise. That was something I hadn't known about my uncle. "Where did you hear that?"

"One of the ladies in her bridge club told me. Seems Ms. Landry loved to fill this group in with the details of her love life."

I giggled. It was hard for me to imagine someone Ms. Landry's age having a love life, but I guess she must have had quite a good one. Most likely better than mine, anyway.

"In fact, she had a plan up her sleeve to get him to marry her," he added.

"A plan?" I asked, only knowing one thing that would force a guy to get married, and that one didn't work after a certain time in a woman's life. "What could she have possibly done to force Uncle Bing to marry her?"

With a shake of his head, Jerry replied, "She had some information on your uncle that he didn't want anyone else to know about."

Leaning back in my chair, I racked my brain to think of something, some dark secret, anything Uncle Bing could possibly have done that he'd want to keep a secret. Nothing came to mind.

With a frown, I asked, "Like what, for instance?"

Jerry let out a long sigh. "We're not sure yet. And we're not sure who else might have known his secret." He sipped his drink before adding, "Or even if there really is a secret."

"This is beginning to sound ridiculous, like a bad movie," I finally said. "You don't think my uncle committed the murder, and I *know* he didn't." I was beginning to rethink the wisdom of keeping him locked up. "Why don't you let him go so he can get on with his life? Besides, if he's out of jail, maybe he can help find who really did this."

"I already told you," Jerry said, his voice tinged with a note of frustration, "he might be in danger if we let him go free."

"Oh, yeah." Now I remembered. "That's right." I

also knew Uncle Bing would try to help out with the investigation, and that would slow us way down.

"And if the real murderer thinks we're not looking that hard for anyone else in the case, he might get careless."

I understood what the captain was doing now. Smug criminals often did stupid things. But still, how could we justify keeping Uncle Bing behind bars once it was obvious the evidence wouldn't hold up?

"What's your next move?" I asked, thinking that since Jerry had told me so much already, he wouldn't mind sharing a little more about the case.

He chuckled as he swirled the ice around in his tea glass. "I'm surprised at you, Miss Walsh. You've been in law enforcement long enough to know better than to think I'll tell you something like that."

"But—" I said before he leveled me with his squinty-eyed cop look.

"If and when the information becomes public knowledge, I'll tell you. Until then, only people involved in the investigation are privy to what's going on."

I let my breath out in a disgusted whoosh. Jerry had just said fighting words as far as I was concerned. My competitive nature and my cop instincts kicked into high gear, and I was now determined to do my own investigative work. He wasn't going to best me on this case. After all, what could a Gulfside cop do that I couldn't do better?

Leaning forward on his forearms, Jerry looked at me from beneath his heavy brows. "And I don't want you getting any ideas of your own about how to handle this." He clamped his mouth shut for a minute before he added, "You understand?"

I folded my arms with my elbows resting on the table, grinning like a troll doll. Nothing was better than silence for getting the goat of a cop in control—or one who thought he was, anyway.

Without any warning, Jerry stood and tapped his fingers on the table, letting me know he was ready to leave. I hated the way he said and did things that threw me off-guard.

On our way out of the restaurant, I glanced over my shoulder and caught the eye of Alice, Bonita Landry's daughter. She was nervous, I could tell. But I didn't let on. I just smiled and turned back to face where I was going. Good thing, too, because Jerry had stopped to pay the bill, and if I'd kept watching behind my back, I would have run smack dab into him.

He took me back to the station where I'd parked my car. "Want me to follow you home?" he asked.

I laughed out loud. "Now why would you want to do something like that?"

"You might need protection," he replied.

"Look, Jerry," I said slowly. "I was a cop for a long time. I know how to protect myself, even if the bad guy tries to hurt me."

"Are you sure?"

With a snort, I backed away from him. "Positive. Now let me get back so I can get some rest. I have a lot to do tomorrow."

"Don't take any action you don't clear with me first," he warned.

Again, I smiled with my mouth closed and my eyes drooping. I knew I looked pretty goofy, but he was treating me like I didn't have a lick of sense. If he thought I was going to sit back and not do a thing before discussing it with him first, he was the fool, not me.

When I went inside, I saw the message light blinking on the answering machine. Who would have called Uncle Bing? Didn't all his friends know where he was?

I crossed the room and pushed the button. It was my mom. She wanted to make sure I'd arrived safely. I let out a sigh and sank down on the chair beside the telephone. She deserved a phone call, even if I did have to break this awful news to her. I knew she'd worry even more, but if I didn't tell her what was going on, she'd be spittin' mad later, after it was all over.

My mother's reaction was exactly what I thought it would be. "Oh, Summer, why does trouble have to follow you everywhere you go?" See? It was all about me. She wasn't worried that someone had been murdered. "Why don't you come back home, and we can help you decide what to do next?"

"Mom," I said, drawing out the single syllable word. "In case you didn't hear me, I told you, Uncle Bing is in jail. He's been accused of murder."

"I know, honey, but he's a grown man. He can take

care of himself. If he didn't do it, he has nothing to worry about."

"Don't be naive, mom," I said. "There are tons of people in jail who are innocent. It's my duty to help him."

"But you once told me you were always certain that when you locked up a criminal that they were guilty," she said.

"I'm not the one who locked him up, Mom. These cops here do things differently, and I need to stick around to make sure Uncle Bing gets a fair shake."

"D-do you think he might have had anything to do with it?" she stuttered, now sounding like the magnitude of what had happened might have sunk in.

"Come on, Mom, you've known Uncle Bing all your life. What do you think?"

"Well, there was that time he pushed me in the ditch," she said. Then, she cleared her throat. "But he helped pull me out when I started screaming. No, of course he didn't have anything to do with it."

I rolled my eyes as my mother worked through this in her own sweet, naive way. Finally, I said, "I need to get off now. Tomorrow I have a mile-long list of things to do."

"Just try to stay out of trouble, sweetie," she said. "Tell Bing we love him and we hope he gets better soon."

I had to laugh when I hung up. My mother was the type of housewife who obsessed over which detergent got the most stains out of her clothes. Murder was something that only happened to other people. I had a feeling she still didn't realize how much trouble her brother was in, or she would have been on the next plane to Florida. It was probably good that she didn't know.

That night I went to bed with a legal pad propped on my lap and a stack of pillows behind my head. I had no intention of falling asleep right away, but after listing two suspects and everything I knew about them, I must have dozed off. When I awoke, I was hanging off the bed with the notepad crumpled and the pen lying on the floor beneath my hand that was dangling from the edge.

It took me nearly an hour to regain full range of motion from all the thrashing around I must have done in my sleep. I'd hoped for a long, restful vacation, but it wasn't gonna happen as long as Uncle Bing was the primary suspect.

The shower felt good. Uncle Bing had invested in a massaging shower head that relieved some of the tension in my shoulders.

As I emerged from the bathroom, the phone was ringing. I managed to catch it before it stopped.

"Summer?" It was Uncle Bing. "Can you come pick me up?"

"What?" I dropped the towel and reached for my robe that I'd draped over the doorknob. "You're out of jail?"

"That Chief of Police finally let me go. I can't be-lieve they kept me as long as they did." His voice cracked. I have to admit, it was good to know he was no longer behind bars, although I suspected everything would take double the effort now that I had help.

"When can you leave?" I asked.

"Now." He sounded urgent.

"Let me get dressed, and I'll be right there."

"Good girl. Maybe now we can figure out who killed Bonita." I heard the anguish in his voice that let me know just how much he really had cared for the murdered woman.

"Don't say or do anything until I get there, Uncle Bing. Just sit quietly."

"Trust me," he said in a gruff voice, "I have nothing to say to these people."

As soon as I hung up, I threw on some jeans and a t-shirt. That was one good thing about Florida. No one expected people to dress up for anything.

Captain Jerry Stokes wasn't in his office when I got there. The day shift was in. I wondered if Jerry was aware of Bing's release, but I didn't ask. I wasn't sure how they operated or if I needed to be careful of office politics.

The instant Uncle Bing got into his car, he started talking ninety miles an hour. "First stop, the bank." He thrust his finger in front of my face. "Turn here."

I did what I was told. "Why are we going to the bank?"

"It's Bonita's bank. I wanna make sure her account is still intact."

"Wait a minute, Uncle Bing," I said. "They're not gonna tell you how much money is in her account." I didn't tell him I knew he was on Ms. Landry's account. I wanted to see if he'd volunteer the information.

"Yes, they will," he said. "It's in both of our names."

I smiled. What a relief. My uncle hadn't changed. He was still the same open person he always was.

Uncle Bing nodded. "She was worried that her daughter would have her ruled incompetent, so she asked me to do this, just in case."

"When did this happen?" I asked.

He chewed on his lip for a few seconds before he replied, "It was one day last week . . . let's see. I think it was Tuesday."

"But I heard that her son-in-law was looking over her books and saw higher amounts than she actually had. Why did she wait?"

Uncle Bing shrugged. "I'm not sure, but I do know one thing: she entrusted me with this money, and I'm not gonna let her down."

I inhaled through my nose and let the breath out from puffed cheeks. It didn't look good for Uncle Bing at the moment. As soon as Jerry caught wind that Uncle Bing had stopped off at the bank, he'd most certainly throw Uncle Bing back behind bars and have even more reason to do it. Instead of stopping in the parking lot, I drove right through to the other side.

"Where are we going?" Uncle Bing asked. "I wanted to go in and check Bonita's account."

"Not now," I said, staring straight ahead at the road before me. It was tempting to keep driving all the way back to Nashville. "Not any time today."

"And why not?" he asked. "What if that no-good Alice cleaned out Bonita's account?"

"How can she do that if your name's on it?"

"I don't know," he said. "But I think she might have an old will from years ago, before she married Barney."

"We don't need to worry about Alice and Barney wiping out her bank account."

Uncle Bing shook his head. "That's not what Bonita wanted."

"Then let me put it another way. If they did that already, what can you do about it?" I asked him, still not turning to look at him.

"I can go have a talk with Alice."

How could Uncle Bing be so naive? "You think she'll talk to you?"

He shrugged. "I don't see why not. I never did anything to her."

"She might see things differently," I suggested. "Being the other signature on her mother's bank account might seem like a threat to her."

"Maybe," he said with a shrug. "But sometimes people will talk when you reason with them."

"I have a feeling she's not in the mood to reason with you, Uncle Bing. At least not while you're a suspect in her mother's murder."

We rode along in silence for a few minutes. Uncle Bing was still pouting over the fact that I wouldn't stop at the bank, but I didn't care. He and I needed to have a long talk first.

"I didn't do it, Summer."

"You already told me that."

"You do believe me, don't you?"

"Of course I do," I said. "But we have to prove that you didn't."

"Whatever happened to being innocent until proven guilty?"

I let out another exasperated sigh as I turned into his condo parking lot. "The way things look right now, Uncle Bing, they could lock you away, throw away the key, and be justified in doing it."

"I still don't understand," he said.

"There's something I don't understand, Uncle Bing." As much as I hated to bring this up, I knew it needed to be out in the open. "What did Bonita have on you that you didn't want other people to know about?"

Uncle Bing's face turned white as a sheet. "You don't need to know that, Summer."

"Well, maybe not, but someone's gonna find out soon, and you might need me."

"Okay," he said. "There was a time when Delta called me in the middle of the night to help her with a problem."

I lifted one eyebrow and studied him for a second. "Was that the night her ex-husband saw you crawling out of her window?"

Uncle Bing nodded. "Yeah, but I shouldn't have done that. Made me look guilty."

"Were you guilty of anything?"

"No, not at all. I just made a mistake and listened

to Delta. I think she wanted to make Henry jealous. She knew he'd see me."

"He thinks something was going on between you. In fact, he told the cops that you killed Bonita when she confronted you with it."

"Then we just have to find out who killed her," he said, as if I hadn't thought of that already.

"I'm working on it."

"Any leads?"

Nodding, I told him about the people I'd met. He just sat in silence and listened, even after I turned off the ignition. Finally, after I told him everything I knew about everyone, he turned to me and shook his head.

"None of those people did it, Summer," he said.

"Come on, Uncle Bing," I tried to reason. "They all had a motive. Is there someone else?"

He steepled his fingers and stared at them for a few seconds before turning to face me. "A lot of people didn't care for Bonita. She had a way of teasing men and making women jealous. And that daughter of hers is a real piece of work. I have no idea how such a selfish snob could have come from someone as fine as Bonita."

"But I thought Ms. Landry was a big tease," I said. "Sounds to me like you liked her. A lot."

Uncle Bing nodded. "I did. She and I were two peas in a pod. Of course, you know I'd never be one to settle down, but if I ever did, she's the one I would have wanted."

"You're kidding. You would have married someone you couldn't trust?"

With a chuckle, he said, "I'd never take my eyes off her for a minute, and I'd enjoy the view."

"Pretty, huh?" I couldn't help but smile at the thought of my confirmed bachelor uncle being in love, which he'd obviously been with this Ms. Bonita Landry.

"Stunning. Even at her age, she could turn heads and make men swoon."

"No wonder the women didn't like her. But what about Alice? Why the rift between them?"

"Bonita didn't like Barney. She called him a money-grubbing, good-for-nothing loser."

"That about sums up everything I've heard about him."

"You gotta meet him," Uncle Bing said. "He's the type to sell swamp land to poor little old ladies who don't have two nickels to rub together."

"I have met him."

Uncle Bing's head snapped around, and he glared at me. "You went to see them?"

"No," I replied. "I saw them at the Barefoot Bar and Grille last night."

"How did you find out about that place?" Uncle Bing asked. "It's not exactly the most famous restaurant in town."

I should have been more prepared for this. Now I had to tell him that Captain Jerry Stokes and I had gone out for dinner, and I wasn't sure what his reaction would be.

"I, uh," I began.

He narrowed his eyes as he leaned toward me. "You

what, Summer? Speak up. You know I don't like you
to mumble."

Squaring my shoulders and looking him directly in
the eye, I said, "Captain Stokes and I went there last
night to discuss your case."

He grinned from ear to ear. "So you're gonna do it,
huh?"

Now I was confused. "I'm gonna do what?"

With a bobbing head, Uncle Bing chuckled. "Captain Stokes told me he was going to get you involved,
but I told him you were retired from police work. I
guess he was right about you."

"What?" I'd gotten the impression that Jerry didn't
want me involved.

"He told me 'once a cop, always a cop,' and I guess
he was right."

So I'd been manipulated. Jerry had known all along
that the more resistance he gave the more I'd want to
help out. I didn't like the idea of this, but I wasn't
about to disappoint my uncle. I'd wait until this whole
thing was over, and I'd let Captain Jerry Stokes know
how I felt.

"Back to Bonita's daughter and her husband Barney," Uncle Bing reminded me. "You said you saw
them last night. What did they say?"

"Not much," I replied. "At least nothing I could
gather that would incriminate them."

"You think they might have done it?" he asked.

"It's possible. Looks to me like they're pretty mo-
tivated by money."

Uncle Bing chuckled. "The paltry sum that Bonita

had in her account wouldn't have been enough to knock her off, even though she thought she was rich."

"Did she give anyone the impression she had a lot?" I asked.

"She tried to, but I don't think anyone believed her. In fact, she owed everyone in town, including me." Uncle Bing paused for a moment to think. Then, he said, "She altered the numbers in her bank books before Barney took a look at it."

"Yeah, I already heard about that."

"You did?" Uncle Bing quickly turned to glare at me. "Who else knew?"

"Everyone."

Uncle Bing shook his head in sadness. "One of Bonita's problems was that she talked too much."

"What about Alice and Barney? Did she ever convince them she didn't have the kind of money she'd initially led them to believe she had?"

"I don't think so. When they came to borrow money from her, she told them she didn't have half of what they were asking for. They left her condo so fast, your head would spin."

"Did they say anything?"

Uncle Barney shrugged. "Barney called Bonita a tightwad."

"I wonder what Alice sees in him," I said. "He's not particularly attractive, and from what I've heard, he didn't waste any time mourning his first wife's death."

With a chuckle, Uncle Bing replied, "Barney buys

her what she wants, but I have a feeling he expects something in return."

I raised an eyebrow at him. "What could he possibly want from Alice?"

"He most likely wanted what he thought she had, and I'll lay you odds he's disappointed that she can't deliver."

"Her mother's money?" I asked.

"Bingo."

We were still sitting in the car talking. I'd noticed several shades and curtains pulled to the side, obviously curious people who had nothing better to do than monitor the parking lot. Uncle Bing saw me staring at the building, and he turned around to see what I was looking at.

"What the—?" he said before opening the door and bolting from the car.

Chapter Eight

I was so stunned by Uncle Bing's reaction, I didn't have time to move before he was gone. He'd obviously seen something that bothered him, and he wasn't going to take the time to tell me what it was. I knew then that I couldn't waste a single second. I had to get out and find out what was going on.

"Uncle Bing!" I shouted as I raced toward him. "Wait up!"

He motioned for me to go back. "Not now, Summer." Then, he raised his fingers to his lips to shush me. "Let me handle this."

"Handle what?" No way was I going to let him handle anything by himself, especially after what he'd just been through. Being a prime suspect in a murder case meant that he was being watched through a magnifying glass.

I managed to get to him in time to join him on the elevator. "Someone's in Bonita's condo," he said as he punched the floor number on the panel.

"Are you sure?"

Nodding, he rubbed his chin. "Yeah, Bonita used to sit at her window and watch for me. When I looked up, she always blew me a kiss. I'll never forget her pretty face shining from the inside looking out."

Man, my uncle had it bad. I'd never seen him like this before. I wondered if my mom had any idea how close her brother had been to falling in love, something Uncle Bing swore he'd never do.

"So what are you planning to do?" I asked as the elevator came to a stop and the doors parted.

"I'm gonna go see who's in there," he stated matter-of-factly.

"Oh, no you're not," I said, pulling him by the arm. "We're calling the cops."

"A lotta good that'll do," he said. "They had me locked up for two days, thinking I killed her."

"They still think you killed her," I informed him. "You're just out temporarily because they didn't have enough evidence."

"So they don't know for sure who did it, right?" he asked, pausing for a split second to glance at me.

"They think they know, and they think it's you."

"Then I'd better find out who really did do it, and fast. Just don't get in my way, Summer." He'd stepped out of the elevator and was heading down the hall in the direction of Ms. Landry's condo. I had to skip to keep up with him.

"I am not getting out of your way, and I won't let you do this. We're calling the cops, and that's final." This time, I grabbed my uncle and pulled him back, using all my strength and the technique I'd had to employ when apprehending a criminal.

When he came to a complete stop, he turned and glared at me. "Summer, you can't do this. My life's on the line, and I'm not about to spend more time in jail for a murder I didn't commit."

I tried to reason with him. "Look, Uncle Bing, I know you didn't do it. And that's why I'm sticking around. But this isn't the way to nail the real killer."

He placed his hands on his hips and gave me a look I'd seen on my mother's face. "Just what *is* the way to nail the killer?"

"We have to outsmart this person. We can't let them catch us off guard."

"That's what I'm trying to do now," he said as he took off again, now that I'd loosened my hold on his arm.

Reaching out to grab ahold of him again, I jerked him to a halt. "Oh, no you're not. We're going to your place and calling the authorities."

I saw Uncle Bing's attention being diverted, his face growing white as a sheet. Something was going on behind me.

Whipping around, I found myself face to face with Tom Masterson, the tennis pro, coming out of Ms.

Landry's condo. He looked like he'd been caught with his hands in the cookie jar.

"What are you doing in Bonita's place, Masterson?" Uncle Bing asked, taking advantage of my state of shock to pull away from me. "You have no business even being near this building."

The tennis pro cleared his throat and looked squarely at my uncle, which surprised me. "I'm just getting what's mine."

"How did you get in there?" Uncle Bing asked. I had to admit, he was good at taking advantage of the moment.

"With this," he replied, holding up a key.

"Who gave you that key?" Man, Uncle Bing was gunning those questions so fast, you'd think he was a cop.

"Ms. Landry did," he replied, "when she first started taking tennis lessons from me. She suggested I come up sometime for a drink, and she just happened to drop this in front of me." With a shrug after a moment of silence, he added, "I had no desire to do that when she was alive, but I had to get some of the things she borrowed."

"Like what?" Uncle Bing asked as he got right in the tennis pro's face.

He was doing so well at this interrogation, I wasn't about to interrupt. What fascinated me was the fact that Uncle Bing was so determined to find the real killer, he didn't seem worried about Masterson carrying a gun. But I was.

"Uncle Bing," I said, coming up from behind him. "Let me take over from here."

Tom Masterson grinned like he thought that was a good idea. "Yeah, why don't you let the little woman take over. She's pretty smart for a female."

I felt the blood rushing to my head with that comment. What a jerk! "I think you should save those comments for the cops when they arrive," I said. Then, I leaned toward Uncle Bing, never taking my eyes off Masterson. "Why don't you go to your place and call the cops? I think we've just busted someone for burglary."

"I'm not a burglar," Masterson said, as he darted his eyes from side to side in what I presumed to be an attempt to find a way out. "I've already told you, I had to get something that was mine."

"You're not supposed to let yourself into a place that's not yours. That's called breaking and entering," I said. "Besides, if they find your fingerprints on anything, you know you'll be hauled in for questioning."

"Don't forget the fact that I have the key," he said, holding it up again.

I let out a breath. "People have keys to places they're not supposed to. How do we know you're telling the truth?"

He flashed an evil grin. "You'll just have to trust me."

Trust was the last thing I'd ever have for this guy. From the moment I met him, I had a bad feeling, kind of like a gnawing sensation in my gut that told me to watch over my shoulder and make sure he's not following.

"If you know what's good for you, you'll stay out of Bonita's condo," Bing piped up. He'd grown so quiet for the past few seconds, I thought he might actually understand how important it was for him to keep a low profile. I should have known better.

I gently leaned toward him and nudged him with my elbow, never once taking my eyes off Tom Masterson. He was giving me the creeps, the way he looked at us as if he might have plans for something. I wondered if he had an alibi for the time when Ms. Landry was murdered. I'd have to check that out later. But now, I needed to make sure he didn't go back into her condo.

Taking a step forward, I pointed my finger in an authoritative gesture. "You've obviously already done what you need to do, Mr. Masterson. Now I suggest you go back to your tennis lessons. My uncle and I have things to do."

He glanced back and forth between Uncle Bing and me, then began to edge toward the elevator. We watched in silence as he left.

"Do you think he did it?" Uncle Bing asked me in a voice that sounded like that of a hopeful little boy. "He resented the fact that Bonita didn't like to pay him for what she considered inferior lessons."

"Then why did she keep going back to him?" I asked.

"He's the only tennis instructor at the club."

That didn't sound like a good enough reason to me,

but then I had never been retired with too much time on my hands, either. "So whaddya think?" he asked again. "Is Masterson the murderer?"

With a shrug, I shook my head. "I'm not sure. He'd be an obvious suspect, but the motive doesn't seem strong enough. I'd think Mr. Masterson would cut off her lessons before he'd kill her."

"I agree," he drawled in a doubtful tone. "But he's not exactly the most upstanding citizen in Gulfside. You know he was hired because he has connections."

"So I've heard." My head snapped around so I could look directly at Uncle Bing. "Do you think Ms. Landry was involved with Mr. Masterson in something besides tennis lessons?"

"I don't think so, but I do know that he's pretty good friends with her son-in-law," he told me.

"Why didn't you tell me this before?"

Uncle Bing got a goofy look on his face. "I didn't think it was an issue. People in Gulfside know each other. It's a small town, and you'd have to expect two people like that to be friends, or at least acquaintances."

I wished my uncle would quit trying to think on his own. This was the kind of thing that would hold back the investigation. No matter, though, because I had to call Captain Stokes with the information about running into Tom Masterson. Glancing at my watch, I saw that it would be another hour before Jerry was on duty. The daytime shift was on duty now, so I decided to wait. I wasn't sure I could trust anyone besides Jerry. And in spite of how much of a nuisance I considered him at first, I felt like he meant well, and he wanted to do the right thing.

Uncle Bing and I waited in his condo. He went to his room and came out, saying, "Have you been sleeping in my bed?"

"Only one night," I replied, feeling like Goldilocks talking to one of the bears. "But I got all my stuff out. Is everything okay?"

He grinned back at me. "Everything's fine. It's just that the pillows are flip-flopped."

I remembered how my mother had once told me that Uncle Bing was persnickety about everything, and he had a photographic memory. Surely, we'd be able to use it to solve this case, I thought. The only problem with that, though, was that he wasn't very good at keeping his mouth shut. I'd much rather have him stay out of it than help me if he insisted on talking when it was best to remain silent.

We drank tea and waited for the night shift to arrive at the police station. Then, I called the number on Jerry's card. It was the direct line to his office, so he answered on the first ring.

"Why didn't you tell me Uncle Bing was being released?" I asked in a hushed tone. My uncle had left the room for a moment, and I used this opportunity to dial the number.

"I didn't know it until I got in this afternoon," he replied in a weary tone. "Someone should have spoken to me first. I'm not so sure this is good."

"I know what you mean, but something else has come up, and that's why I called." I told him what had happened when we arrived at the condo building. He was silent as I explained how Tom Masterson had been snooping around Ms. Landry's condo.

"Do you think he did it?" he asked.

"Not really," I replied, "but you have to admit, it is strange for him to let himself into the apartment of a dead woman, especially since her place is being watched."

"That's what I think," he stated. "Any idea how he got in?"

"He has the key."

"How'd he get the key?" he shrieked.

"Says she gave it to him."

"And I don't suppose anyone else knew about it, either," he said, his voice dropping.

"No, I don't think anyone else did."

"Do you believe him?" he asked. In spite of my earlier resentment of Captain Jerry Stokes, I appreciated the fact that he listened to me now. He seemed to respect my cop instincts.

"Yes, I do," I admitted after a brief pause. Although Tom Masterson made my skin crawl, he didn't look like he'd been lying. "I can't imagine why Ms. Landry would have given him her key, but then he was there during the day, when it was likely someone would see him coming or going from her place."

"Yeah," he agreed. "And everyone there knows who he is. It would be impossible for Tom Masterson to move around Gulfside Country Club without someone recognizing him."

"That's exactly what I was thinking."

"Did he have anything in his hands?" he asked.

"Just a tennis racket, but he always has one of those."

"Maybe he was just curious," Jerry offered. "I'll have someone check it out, but I don't want to list him as a suspect just yet."

Uncle Bing chose that moment to come back into the room. "Is that Captain Stokes?" he whispered.

I nodded and motioned for him to be quiet. Jerry told me he planned to keep a close eye on Gulfside Country Club Condos on the Green, just in case someone did something to sabotage the investigation. "I just wish we still had your uncle in custody," he said.

"Me, too," I agreed, trying my best not to let Uncle Bing know what I was talking about.

When we hung up, Uncle Bing was grinning from ear to ear. "You like this Captain Jerry Stokes guy, don't you, Summer?"

I lifted one shoulder and said, "He's okay. A decent cop."

He chuckled. "I think it's more than that, but if you want to act coy, it's your prerogative. You're a woman."

One thing I really appreciated about Uncle Bing was the fact that he never looked at me like I was a little girl, once I'd grown up. I couldn't say the same about my other relatives. Most of them still thought I wanted dolls for Christmas.

"Is he stopping by this evening?" Uncle Bing asked as if this were a normal day of vacation.

"He's on duty, Uncle Bing, and I don't think he'll be here unless he has a reason."

"Trust me, Summer. He'll think of a good reason to be here." Uncle Bing wiggled his eyebrows. "I've seen how he looks at you."

My face heated up instantly, and I had to quickly turn away to keep him from seeing how red I was. Then the phone rang.

"Get that for me, will you, Summer?" Uncle Bing said as he turned and headed toward the hall.

I picked up the phone on the second ring. "Hello, Miss Walsh? This is Alice Hunt. You know, Bonita Landry's daughter? I was wondering if you might be so kind as to meet with me at the Grille a little later on?"

Chapter Nine

First of all, I never expected to hear from Alice Hunt again. And secondly, was that a southern accent I heard? "Uh, sure, Mrs. Hunt," I replied, "I'll be glad to. Are you talking about the Barefoot Bar and Grille?"

"Why, yes," she replied, drawling out both words. "I'll buy you some dinner if that's all right."

I glanced over at Uncle Bing. He and I hadn't mentioned what we were going to do for dinner, but I'd assumed we'd eat out somewhere of his choosing. However, I thought I might better go along with Alice.

"Sounds fine," I said. "What time?"

"How about in two hours?" she said. "Barney is leaving with a few of his friends for the dog tracks, so I thought it might be kind of fun for you and me to get to know one another."

I had no idea why she thought we should become friends, but I wasn't about to argue now. In fact, she was on my list of people to talk to. She'd caught me off guard with her invitation. I'd expected to have a difficult time connecting with her.

"Do you have to?" Uncle Bing whined. "I was looking forward to the two of us going out tonight."

I had to laugh at him, acting so pitiful. Leaning over to give him a quick peck on the cheek, I said, "I won't be out late. I can either bring you something back, or I can fix dinner for you before I leave."

He chewed on his bottom lip while he moped and thought for another minute. Then, on the edge of a deep sigh, he said, "I'll just run out and pick up some fast food. We can talk when you get back."

Since I'd been wearing the same clothes all day, and the heat and humidity had taken its toll on me, I headed for the shower. I needed to freshen up so I could concentrate on what I had to do, which was to get information from Alice without her realizing what I was doing. This had become my specialty back in Nashville.

Uncle Bing and I still had a half hour before I needed to leave, after I was ready. "Okay, tell me everything you can think of before I go," I told him.

He had to think for a few minutes, but once he got started, he was like a fountain of information about Alice and Barney Hunt. "I don't think the two of them always get along, either," he added.

Tilting my head to one side, I said, "Really? Why do you say that?" I'd noticed how she seemed irritated with her husband the first time I saw them, but I'd put that out of my mind, figuring it was typical for married people to act like that once in a while.

"She was always calling Bonita and complaining about her husband."

"Did she want her mother to do anything about it?" I asked.

Shaking his head, he replied, "Only to listen and lend her a little money while they were waiting for their investment money to arrive."

I'd known people like that in my past—people who had plenty of money, but it was all tied up in investments. And they often took advantage of the fact that I always had cash in my wallet.

"Okay," I said as I stood up to leave. "I think I'm ready to go hear what Alice Hunt has to say."

"Here," Uncle Bing said as he fished in his pocket and pulled out his keys I'd given him back earlier. "Take my car."

"I can take mine," I said, holding my hand up.

"No," he insisted. "My car is much more comfortable. You'll appreciate the air conditioning."

He was right. My car was a sub-compact, and the air conditioning blew hot air for the first fifteen minutes it was on. I reached for the keys.

I was all the way to the foyer when I glanced in the gold-framed mirror on the wall and saw the mess my hair was in. I screeched.

"Whatsamatter, Summer?" Uncle Bing asked as he came running to see about me.

"My hair! Why didn't you tell me my hair looked like Bozo's wig?"

He chuckled. "Everyone's hair looks like that here." Reaching up to touch his own bald spot, he added, "At least those of you who have hair do."

I turned around and stomped off to the bedroom. "Well, I'm not about to go out looking like this. I'm putting my hair up."

It took me a few minutes to get all the loose ends of my hair up in a clip. Since it was so humid outside, I decided not to use hairspray because it would be sticky.

"Okay, I'm leaving now," I said to Uncle Bing as I made my way back to the door.

"Be careful with my car," he warned.

"I'll take good care of it," I said as I shut the door behind me. I was really thankful for the use of Uncle Bing's luxury car. Maybe I'd get something like this once I got settled. I was a little older now, and comfort was becoming increasingly important to me.

The Barefoot Bar and Grille was about a half hour away from the Gulfside Country Club. I had to drive through town, then over a causeway before I reached the little section of beach where there were a few restaurants, an art gallery, and some humongous houses on stilts. It was quite nice with a lovely view, but not a place I'd want to be in a hurricane.

I'd reached the edge of the causeway when I glanced in the rearview mirror and saw a car quickly approaching from behind. It was coming up so fast, I felt my heart pound in my throat as I edged over to the side of the road to let whoever was in such a hurry pass me. No sense in keeping this person from getting there on time, wherever "there" was. People like this needed to leave fifteen minutes earlier so they wouldn't always feel so rushed.

But once the car got right on my bumper, it slowed down. I lowered the window, stuck my arm out, and tried to motion for the driver to go around me, but to no avail. It was impossible to see the person behind the wheel because both cars had tinted windows—Uncle Bing's and the car behind me. I understood why people wanted dark windows in Florida, but it sure did impede communication between drivers.

As I got closer to the causeway, I took a deep breath. It was always a little scary to cross this narrow road with water on both sides for several miles and not much shoulder to speak of. I could only imagine what it would be like to have a flat tire on this stretch, and I was thankful once again for the use of Uncle Bing's car. He kept his automobiles in immaculate condition, so I figured I didn't have anything to worry about. Hopefully, this car behind me wouldn't try to pass me until we got to the other side because it seemed awfully dangerous to do so.

The road sound actually changed once I was on the causeway. It made a low, humming noise as the wheels covered the shell-encrusted pavement. My hands gripped the steering wheel a little tighter, and my pulse quickened just a tad from my nervousness.

Although I'd been a cop, driving wasn't my best thing. In fact, when I'd been on patrol, many of my partners insisted on driving.

I wasn't more than a third of the way over the causeway when I began to relax. There weren't any other cars on the road besides mine and the one behind me, so I figured everything would be just fine.

Right when I began to relax my grip on the steering wheel, I glanced in the rearview mirror and saw that the car had gotten right up on my tail again. Then, it started to move over into the oncoming lane! What was that person thinking?

I moved over to the right as far as I could go while still staying in the lane. I didn't want to move to the shoulder because it was slanted a little toward the water, so I stayed on my side of the line. Hopefully, the person would quickly get around me and then I could take my nice, sweet time. I was a little bit early, anyway.

But the car wasn't passing me. I glanced up to my left when it was parallel with me, letting up on the accelerator a little to give them an opportunity to get around me more quickly. The other car slowed down, too.

Narrowing my eyes to get a better look at the other driver, I realized there was no way I could tell who it was. Both cars had tinted windows, the other one almost totally dark, and the sun had already set, casting an ethereal orange glow over the water and road. I had to turn back to focus on my driving.

Then, suddenly, I felt a bump as the car moved back

over into my lane. My fingers gripped the wheel a little tighter. What was going on? Uncle Bing would be livid, but what could I do?

I sped up a little to get to the other side so I could check out the damage to my uncle's car. The other car gained speed, too, and bumped me again.

No matter what I did—speed up or slow down— the other car was right there beside me. Fear rose to my throat as I realized that the person driving that dark car beside me was trying to run me off the road. I wasn't about to hang around and see what would happen. My cop instincts kicked in, and I knew I was in trouble. I had to get outa there. What I'd first thought was a bad driver who was late for an appointment, I now knew was someone who wanted to scare me. Or even worse, kill me.

With my focus on the road before me, my hands gripping the steering wheel, and my jaw tense, I stomped on the gas pedal and tore away from the car that had just swerved to hit me again. I glanced up in my mirror and saw how I'd taken the other driver by surprise. The car now behind me almost left the road and went into the water. I saw it swerving to correct its position on the road as I pulled further and further away. My heart was still in my stomach.

By the time I reached the Gulf side of the causeway, I'd come to terms with the fact that someone was trying to hurt me. But why?

The Barefoot Bar and Grille was less than a mile down the beach. I pulled into the parking lot and got out to inspect the damage to Uncle Bing's car. It was

Deborah Tisdale

pretty bad. His nice, shiny white luxury sedan was banged up on the driver's side, and there was some very dark blue paint streaked all the way from the front to the back. I didn't look forward to facing him with this.

First thing I did when I got inside was ask for the phone. I'd left in a hurry, and my cell phone was lying on the dresser at Uncle Bing's condo.

I called Captain Stokes. "I'll be right there," he said.

"No, I'm supposed to meet with Alice Hunt. She might clam up if she sees you."

"Look, Summer," he said, using my first name for the first I could remember. "If someone's trying to hurt you, you'll need help."

I forced a nervous laugh. "No one's trying to hurt me, Jerry. Probably just some drunk driver. They probably live out here on the island somewhere. Shouldn't be that hard to find them." I knew better than that, but I didn't want Jerry to come. I could have kicked myself for not waiting to call him.

"No," he said. "I'm coming. It's my job."

"Suit yourself," I replied. I understood that he had to do this, and deep down I was actually thankful. The maniac who almost pushed me into the Gulf needed to be removed from the road. "But don't bother Alice and me."

After I got off the phone, I found a table by the window overlooking the water. Glancing down at my watch, I saw that I still had ten minutes before our designated meeting. I had time to enjoy the view and calm down.

Ten minutes went by and still no Alice. Hmm. She must be the type to show up late.

Since I was so hungry, I went ahead and ordered when she still hadn't shown up fifteen minutes later. Then, I stood up and went to the pay phones in the lobby. Maybe she'd tried to get ahold of me.

"No," Uncle Bing said. "No one called. Why, Summer? Are you okay?"

"Sure," I replied, toying with the idea of warning him about his car but deciding to wait. "I'm fine."

"You sound a little strange, sort of like you're upset about something."

Uncle Bing was definitely a people person. He could read me like a book, even over the phone.

"Alice is late, and I'm concerned that she might have called to either cancel or postpone our meeting."

"If she calls, I'll have you paged," he said. "But I haven't heard anything yet." He sounded weary, but I could understand why, after all he'd been through.

My dinner came, I ate, and then I sat around waiting for another hour. Jerry had arrived, but he'd honored my request to keep his distance. He was sitting next to the wall across the room, watching me the whole time. Alice still wasn't here, and it was two hours past the time she'd asked me to meet her. She must have changed her mind, I figured.

When I stood up to leave, I decided to go over and thank Jerry for coming all the way out here. He watched me cross the room but didn't say a word until I spoke first.

"You really didn't have to stick around," I said. "Did you get a look at Uncle Bing's car?"

Jerry nodded. "It's pretty banged up, Summer," he said with a note of concern in his voice. "I drove around the island, but I didn't see any dark blue cars with dented right sides." He stood up and dropped a few bills on the table. "Ready to leave now?"

I nodded. "You don't have to leave. Go ahead and have dinner."

He looked at me with an unreadable expression. "I'm following you back to the mainland."

"You don't—" I began before he interrupted.

"I said, I'm following you. All the way to the Country Club." His voice was firm, and I could tell there would be no arguing with him now.

With a sigh of resignation, I nodded. "Do whatever you feel you need to do."

Captain Jerry Stokes was right behind me all the way across the causeway. I had to admit, it was comforting to know he was there.

When we got to Uncle Bing's parking lot, Jerry pulled up beside me. "Want me to go inside with you while you break the news to your uncle about his car?"

It was tempting to let him, but I shook my head. "No, I can handle it. He'll be mad, but he'll get over it once he realizes I'm fine."

"You sure?"

"Positive." I waved goodbye to him, then turned and went up to see my uncle, who was waiting by the door.

"Was that Jerry with you down there?" he asked.

"Yes, were you watching?" What I should have

asked was if he saw the damage to his car, but I figured he would have said something if he had.

"I was worried," he replied. "You were gone a long
time."

"Uh, Uncle Bing," I said, motioning to his favorite
chair. "Sit down. We need to talk."

He studied me as he slowly crossed the room and
sat down. "What's on your mind, Summer?" His look
of concern for me touched me deeply. However, I
wasn't so sure how long his concern would last once
he found out about what had happened to his car.

I'd been torn as to what I should tell him. If I said
that someone had tried to run me off the road, he
might get too worried to let me out of his sight. But
if I didn't tell him, he'd be furious with me for being
careless. The choice wound up being an easy one,
though, since I still had work to do on his case.

"I wrecked your car, Uncle Bing," I blurted.

"You what?" he said, his voice cracking. "Are you
okay?" He stood back up, crossed over to the window
and looked out. "I don't see any damage."

"I'm fine. It's on the other side," I said. "The
driver's side."

"What happened?"

After only hesitating a couple of seconds, I
shrugged one shoulder, trying hard to act nonchalant.
"I side-swiped someone."

"How in the world—?" By now his face was growing red. Was it anger? Or worry?

I shook my head and continued, briefly telling him
only a partial truth. "I'm not sure how it happened.

Just carelessness, I s'pose. But I'll pay for the damage."

"Nonsense!" he yelled. "That's what insurance is for." He was mad.

"Okay, I'll call my insurance company first thing in the morning. My policy covers any car I drive, even if it's not mine."

Uncle Bing sank back down in the chair and rubbed his hand across his forehead. "Are you sure you're okay, Summer?" I could tell he was still upset, but he'd quickly resigned himself to the fact that there was nothing he could do about the wreck now. However, I had a feeling he'd never offer to loan me his car again, which was just fine. I couldn't handle the guilt.

We stayed up talking for a few more minutes, but I was exhausted. So I went to bed and lay there, staring up at the ceiling, feeling like a zombie, unable to go to sleep. My thoughts were racing around my mind in a jumbled mess. Who would have wanted to run me off the road?

When I awoke the next morning, I was soaked with sweat from thrashing around all night. My dreams had come in fragments, but every single one of them had ended with the vision of that car trying to force me into the Gulf.

I could hear Uncle Bing moving around in the kitchen. The last thing I wanted to do was face him, but I knew I'd have to eventually, so I figured I might as well get it over with.

"Good morning, Summer," he said with a bright smile on his face. He looked completely different from how he'd looked the night before—a little too cheerful.

"I need some coffee," I said as I headed toward the pot that sat on the kitchen counter. "Did you see the car?"

He nodded. "Yes, I did." He handed me the creamer from the refrigerator and added, "And I spoke with Captain Stokes too."

I let out the breath I just realized I'd been holding. I'd hoped to talk to Jerry before he had a chance to talk to my uncle. "What did he tell you?"

Uncle Bing spun around to face me, a look of concern taking the place of the fake smile he'd worn when I first came out of my room. "Why didn't you tell me someone tried to run you off the road, Summer?"

I hung my head in my hands. "I didn't want to worry you."

"It didn't work," he said in a crisp tone. "I knew something wasn't right when you told me about the wreck. You acted like it was nothing, and I just happen to know it's not like you to be so lackadaisical. I want you to be honest with me from now on. Otherwise, how can we catch who killed Bonita?"

The pain in his voice was evident. Not only had he lost the woman he loved, he now felt like he couldn't trust me.

"I'm sorry, Uncle Bing. That was a mistake."

"A huge mistake," he agreed. "Captain Stokes is coming over in about an hour. He has a lead on the car that side-swiped you."

My head shot up. "He does?"

Nodding, Uncle Bing went on. "Your Captain Stokes is on the ball. After he left the Grille last night, he put out a bulletin to all the auto body shops in the area, and first thing this morning he got a call from one of them. He didn't have all the information yet, but he's going to have it before he comes this morning."

I glanced at the wall clock. It was still morning, which meant Jerry probably hadn't gotten any sleep. I felt awful, knowing that I'd caused him so much worry.

After a quick English muffin with marmalade and a cup of coffee, I showered and got ready to see Jerry. Uncle Bing let him in and made small talk until I came back out.

Both men looked up at me when I entered the room, and I got a huge dose of open admiration. It felt good, but I didn't think I deserved it.

"Whatcha got?" I asked Jerry as soon as I sat down on the sofa.

Shaking his head, he said, "You're not gonna believe this, but I think we just solved everything because of this."

"Everything?" I asked.

He changed the direction of his head and began to nod. "Barney Hunt is the man."

"Barney Hunt?" How could that be? Wasn't he supposed to have gone to the tracks with his friends?

"Yeah, when I got the call from Al's Body Shop, he gave me the name and address of the owner of the navy blue Oldsmobile with tinted windows. It's Barney Hunt."

Chapter Ten

"Why would he want to run me off the road?" I asked, puzzled about all this. I'd only met the man once in my life. What did I do to make him mad enough to possibly want to kill me?

"You were in your uncle's car. When we arrested him, he didn't deny he'd done it. But he thought it was your uncle driving. He had no idea he'd almost run you into the Gulf."

That's right. It was dusk, and I'd put my hair up in a clip. Add that to both cars having tinted windows, and it was no wonder he didn't know it was me. But why would he want to run Uncle Bing off the road?

While all this was sinking in, Uncle Bing backed out of the living room, saying, "You might want to tell her the rest now, Captain."

I jerked my head up and glared at Jerry. "The rest?"

He cleared his throat and glared back at my uncle, who quickly left the room. I could tell they were very uncomfortable.

"What's going on?"

Jerry looked down, then back up at me. "Alice was found dead this morning."

"Alice?" I asked, my voice cracking. "Alice Hunt?"

"She was in the garage when our patrol officer arrived to talk to Mr. Hunt. She'd been dead since last night."

"Wait a minute," I said as I stood and began to pace. "I was supposed to meet with Alice, but she didn't show up because someone killed her?"

"Looks that way."

"Oh, man," I said as I sat back down. My knees had just given out when the magnitude of what had happened hit me. I'd been sitting at the restaurant waiting for a dead woman! "Any idea who killed her?"

"We know who murdered Alice," Jerry said slowly, looking directly at me.

"Okay," I said. "Are you gonna tell me, or do I have to drag it out of you?"

He closed his eyes, inhaled deeply, then let his breath out. I could tell it was hard for him to tell me. Finally, he blurted, "Barney."

My ears suddenly started ringing, and the room began to spin. "Barney?"

Jerry nodded. "That's why I'm still working."

I gulped. "One question. Did he try to run me off the road before or after he killed Alice?"

"After."

The impact of knowing that a murderer had tried to kill me right after he'd killed his wife was too much for me to handle at the moment. Sure, I'd apprehended criminals, including cold-blooded murderers, before. But this was directed at me, even though it had been meant for Uncle Bing.

"Why did he want to hurt Uncle Bing?" I asked.

"That's what we're still trying to figure out."

"Barney told you he killed his wife and then tried to run my uncle off the road, but he wouldn't say why?" That sounded strange, even to me, and I'd heard it all.

"He gave us a reason, but I don't buy it," Jerry said. "He said his wife was jealous when she found out he wasn't really going to the dog tracks with his friends. On top of everything else, she refused to tell him who she was meeting, and he got jealous. They had a fight, and when she came after him swinging a golf club, he grabbed it away from her. She wouldn't let up, so he figured he'd knock her around a little to get her to stop."

"He killed her with a golf club?" I asked.

Nodding, Jerry continued. "It only took one hit. He must have quite a swing. One crack to the skull and she was gone. Dead as a doornail."

I shuddered to think about being killed by a golf club. The game would never be the same for me now. "I wonder why she wouldn't tell him who she was meeting," I said softly.

With a shrug, Jerry replied, "Probably because she

wanted to tell you some stuff she didn't want him to know."

"But I don't even know her. Why would she confide in me?"

Uncle Bing was back in the living room by now, and he was the one who answered. "Most likely on account of you're my niece. Alice always had a strange way of doing things."

I looked at my uncle. "Do you think Barney killed Ms. Landry?"

"I've gone back and forth on that," he replied. "At first, I thought it was possible. Then, I figured that since Bonita didn't have any money to speak of, I changed my mind. I never liked the guy, but I couldn't see a reason, even for him, to kill Bonita. Now I'm not so sure."

"That is, unless he thought she was holding back on how much money she really had," Uncle Bing said.

I turned back to Jerry. "What do you think?"

He shrugged. "It's possible. Since Gulfside is such a small community, it's hard for me to imagine more than one murderer running around. But Ms. Landry's and her daughter's murders were completely different."

I puffed out my cheeks and blew out my breath. It appeared that all suspicion was now off my uncle. At least, no one seemed to be pointing the finger at him anymore. I'd noticed that when he first came back home, most of the people walked a wide berth around him, but they'd slowly begun to smile and greet him again.

Then, I thought about something else that was nagging at the back of my mind. "Why would Barney Hunt want to kill Uncle Bing?"

Jerry nervously cleared his throat. "Seems your uncle knows something that could do some damage to him."

I turned to my uncle and stared at him. He suddenly looked very uncomfortable. "Well?" I asked in the most demanding tone I could manage.

"I didn't say anything," he said, looking away.

"No, but you're going to. Why would Barney Hunt want to hurt you—possibly even kill you?"

"I might have seen something," he replied.

"Like what?" I stood up and went over to where he sat on the arm of the sofa. "You have to tell us now."

"Look, Summer, this whole thing is awful embarrassing. It's not good for him or me."

"I don't care, Uncle Bing. I want to know what's going on." I gestured toward Jerry. "He needs this for his investigation. We need to find out who murdered Bonita Landry."

Uncle Bing folded his arms across his chest, rolled his eyes, and then closed them. "Okay, if you must know, I saw him with another woman."

"What was so difficult about that?" I asked, puzzled as to why he was keeping this such a secret.

"Because I was with another woman, too," he spat.

I had to bite my lips to keep from laughing out loud. Uncle Bing didn't have to worry about being with another woman; he wasn't married.

"So, what's the problem?" I asked.

"I was with Delta, Henry's wife," he replied. Okay, now this whole picture looked a lot different.

Now I was confused. "I thought they were divorced."

"Not at the time," my uncle admitted shamefully. "In fact, Delta even proposed to me that night. She told me she'd divorce Henry to marry me." He shuddered as if the very thought of marrying Delta repulsed him.

Jerry and I quickly glanced at each other. "You were with Delta?" Jerry asked in disbelief. "But why?" He didn't have to say another word. I knew what he was thinking.

My uncle nodded with his eyes shut. "I know, I know, it doesn't make sense to be traipsing off with a floozy like Delta when you've got a pretty lady like Bonita back here waiting for you. But I'd had a few drinks, and she came on to me, making me feel pretty special with that German-chocolate cake she'd baked for my birthday. Bonita didn't like it a single bit, but she just fussed over me a little more." He threw his hands up in the air and shuddered. "I have no idea why I did it, except it worked when I was with Maude."

"Maude?" Jerry asked. "You mean the waitress at the Gulfside Grill?" He cast a quick glance at me.

"That's beside the point," I said, interrupting this line of questioning. I'd find out more and tell Jerry about Uncle Bing's escapades with Delta and Maude later. Now, we had more pressing issues. "What's the point of trying to run you off the road just because you were both out with women you weren't supposed to be with?"

Uncle Bing looked at me like a three year old who'd just gotten caught raiding the cookie jar. "Because I told him if he didn't mind his Ps and Qs, I'd tell Alice what he was up to."

I let out a sigh of exasperation. This whole situation kept getting more and more convoluted. "But Alice was already dead. Do you think he killed Bonita?" I asked.

"Who else would do something like that?" Uncle Bing asked.

Then, I remembered. Delta. If she was willing to risk her marriage to Henry to be with Uncle Bing, she was a likely suspect. But it was still hard to imagine the woman with the big black hair strangling someone. Besides, she didn't look strong enough to hurt a flea, let alone kill someone.

Or maybe it was Henry. It was a stretch, but people did strange things out of jealousy. He did seem like a rather odd little man when I first met him.

Could Maude have been the murderer? She sure did flaunt her body around my uncle.

My head now ached with all the possibilities swirling around in my brain. Most people had given up on the notion that Uncle Bing had murdered his lady friend. However, I could tell that he was being watched. I knew for a fact that he'd been advised not to leave town. At least, that's what he'd told me.

Still, though, it appeared that since Barney had admitted guilt to killing his wife, he most likely had taken her mother out too. But something bothered me about that theory. His motive to kill Bonita Landry had been squelched when he found out she wasn't sitting on financial easy street. Uncle Bing thought Barney might have still believed she had money, but I didn't think that was the case. Besides, what good would a poor, dead mother-in-law do him?

After Jerry left Uncle Bing's condo, I went to the kitchen to finish cleaning up. I needed something to do with my hands. For the first time in my life, I was confused about a case, not knowing what to do next.

The cops had Barney Hunt in custody, and they weren't likely to let him go, since he'd admitted to his wife's murder. Uncle Bing and I had a long talk, with him trying to convince me to stay far away from that deadbeat, good-for-nothing piece of trash Bonita's daughter had married. But I was determined to talk to him so I could get a better feel for who might want to kill my uncle.

As soon as the condo was neat and clean, I headed down to the police station. Jerry had already gone home, so I had to deal with someone from the day shift.

"I'm sorry, but he can't see anyone right now," the young guy at the front desk told me.

"Look," I said, shoving my face within inches of his so I could keep my voice low yet still be heard, "I'm helping in this investigation, and I want to see Barney Hunt now."

Shaking his head, he continued trying to hold me back. "I'm sorry, ma'am, but I can't."

"Call Captain Stokes," I ordered. "He'll tell you to let me in."

Hopefully, I was right. I stood there while he dialed Jerry's number. The young officer apologized up one side and down the other for waking Jerry, which made me smile. I had to bite my lips again to keep from laughing when I saw how red his face had gotten.

"Uh, go right on back to the interrogation room, Miss Walsh," he said. "I'll get Mr. Hunt."

I made my way to the room where I'd visited Uncle Bing and found a seat by the window where I could get a good look at Barney Hunt and he'd have to squint into the sunlight that was streaming through the open blinds. I needed to study his face for a few minutes before I could draw any conclusions.

He came into the room and then tried to back out when he saw me sitting there. "No, I'm not going in," he told the officer.

"You have ten minutes," the young cop said, ignoring Mr. Hunt's objection and shoving him inside the room. "I'll be right out here if you need me." He was trying to make amends for putting me off earlier.

I stared at the man for a solid thirty seconds before I nodded toward the seat across from me. "Might as well have a seat. Ten minutes will seem like an hour if you stand there all tense like that."

He snorted. But he sat, just like I'd told him to. I was glad. The very idea of making him squirm in his chair appealed to me much more than watching him shuffle his feet around on the tile floor.

"First of all, Mr. Hunt, I'd like to know why you tried to kill me on the causeway last night," I began.

His dour expression turned into a snicker. "I thought you were Bing. How was I to know you'd be driving that old coot's car?"

I leaned forward and widened my eyes. "Okay, I'll start over. Why were you trying to kill 'that old coot,' my uncle?"

Chapter Eleven

Mr. Hunt shrugged. "I don't like him messing up my life."

"How did he mess up your life?" I asked. His quick response really surprised me. I'd half expected to spend most of my ten minutes trying to get him to warm up. But he was ready to chat.

"He tried to talk Alice into leaving me last time she called her mother. Bonita had the nerve to let him listen in on the extension."

"Sounds to me like you didn't need any help in that department," I offered. "Or hasn't anyone told you that being unfaithful isn't a good way to keep a wife?"

"That's none of your business," he said gruffly.

"Under most conditions, you're right. But when you try to shove me into the Gulf of Mexico, wreck my favorite uncle's car, and then commit murder, then it suddenly becomes my business."

"Your favorite uncle is greedy. Did you know he got his hands on all of Bonita's money?"

I laughed. "What money? From what I understand, there wasn't very much, but you already knew that, didn't you?"

He looked around the room with annoyance, then shook his head. "I don't have to put up with this, Miss Walsh."

"You don't know the half of what you're gonna have to put up with, Mr. Hunt. If you think I'm bad, wait'll you see what my uncle's attorney will do to you."

"Your uncle's attorney?" he asked.

"Yeah, for wrecking his car." I paused for effect, then added, "And attempted murder." With the most smug look I could manage, I added, "After your admission to murdering Alice, you know the cops would love more ammunition to take to court."

He groaned out loud, burying his face in his hands. I'd gotten to him. When he pulled his hands away from his face, I saw how pale it was. Good. Served him right to feel awful. I had no sympathy for anyone who murdered, unless it was in self-defense, which, considering his size, wasn't the case with his wife.

"What do you want from me, Miss Walsh?" he finally asked.

I leaned forward and studied him for a moment before I said, "Did you kill Bonita Landry?"

"No, I didn't," he replied. And for some reason, I believed him. But I couldn't let him know that.

"So you're saying you were jealous and angry enough to kill your wife, but you didn't care enough about your inheritance to murder your mother-in-law?"

"That's exactly what I'm saying," he said with conviction. "Besides, you just said yourself that the old hag didn't have two nickels to rub together."

"You're exaggerating, Mr. Hunt. There's no room for that when you're on the stand in court."

"How would you know?" he asked. "Are you an attorney, or something?"

"No," I replied, waiting a few seconds to catch him off guard. "I'm a cop."

The groan that came from his throat was so loud, the young police officer outside the door stuck his head in and said, "You okay, Miss Walsh?"

"I'm just fine," I replied as I stood to leave, "but I think Mr. Hunt might be starting to tire. Take him back to his cell."

Nothing like the elements of surprise and disappointment, I thought. I figured it would take Barney Hunt a day or two of thinking and reflecting before he could come to grips with what I'd told him about my past career. And maybe next time he wouldn't be so eager to take matters into his own hands to protect his greedy self.

Uncle Bing was hovering by the front door, ready to pounce on me when I got back to his condo. "Well?" he asked. "How'd it go?"

I shrugged and moved past him to the kitchen. My mouth was parched; I needed something to drink.

"Come on, Summer, tell me," he demanded, following me into the kitchen like a small child. "The guy tried to kill you, thinking you were me, and now you're giving me the silent treatment? I have a right to know."

"He didn't say much of anything, Uncle Bing." I'd poured a glass of water and was now leaning against the kitchen counter, drinking it, facing him.

"Something must have happened. Barney Hunt has something up his sleeve. If he killed Bonita—"

"Don't assume he's the one who killed her," I interrupted.

"If he did that to his own wife, then, don't you think he might have strangled Bonita?"

"Not necessarily."

"So you don't think he did it?" Uncle Bing asked.

"I didn't say that," I replied. "What I'm saying is that I still don't know for sure. It could have been him, but then again it could have been any number of people. From what I can tell, there are quite a few folks around here who don't miss her a single bit."

"I miss her," he said softly.

"Yes, I know you do." I quickly placed my water glass on the counter and crossed the room to comfort my uncle who was standing there looking dejected. It broke my heart to see him so lonely like this. I'd had no idea things were this way for him, but I suspected it hadn't just started. He'd probably been feeling lonely for a long time and covered it up by talking like a big shot when we called.

"Who else do you think it could have been?" Uncle Bing asked.

"Well, there's Clyde Bullhouser. He was very jealous, you know." I held up one finger. Then, I lifted another finger and said, "And how about Delta or her ex-husband Henry?" A third finger went up.

Uncle Bing nodded. "I can't imagine any of those people murdering anyone, but I've seen all their bad sides. Things can get pretty ugly with all of them when they don't get their way."

I lifted a fourth finger. "How about Tom Masterson? There's something about that man that really gets on my nerves."

With a shudder, Uncle Bing agreed. "I know what you mean. But I don't think he did it."

"So that makes five suspects," I said. "But I don't think the tennis pro did it, either, so we're down to four."

He looked confused. "I thought that left only two. Who are the other two?"

"Don't forget Barney. He's not off the hook." Then, I swallowed hard and took a long look at my uncle before I added, "And you're still a suspect, even though they let you out of jail."

"I am?" he asked, a shocked expression covering his face. "I thought they knew I didn't do it."

I shook my head and did my best to explain it to him. "They have evidence on you, but they felt that there were other people just as likely to have committed the crime."

"Oh," he simply said as he rubbed his chin. "I didn't realize they still thought I did it."

"Well, I for one don't think you did it," I said to comfort him. "I've known you all my life, and I can't imagine you ever hurting anyone."

"Especially Bonita," he said, smiling and hugging me. "And I'd never hurt you or let you down, either, Summer. You've always been my favorite niece."

That warm, loving moment didn't last long. The phone rang, jolting us from our hug. It was Clyde Bullhouser. I'd wondered what he was up to, since I hadn't heard from him in a while. I knew he was still in town because the cops had told him he'd better stay put.

He wanted to know what was going on. Delta had called and informed him that Barney Hunt was in jail for attempted murder. Uncle Bing corrected that by letting Mr. Bullhouser know that it was a murder charge, and Barney had admitted to it. These people around here sure did get information fast, I thought. During the entire time I'd lived in my apartment in Nashville, I rarely ever saw my neighbors out, let alone know what they did in their spare time or anything about their brushes with the law.

Uncle Bing told him everything he knew. I didn't object because I felt that if Mr. Bullhouser was guilty of anything, he'd be delighted in knowing he was temporarily off the hook, and his guard would drop. I'd have to keep an eye on him, although I knew that no one else considered him a serious suspect. I really didn't, either, but you never know until all the evidence is in.

After having a light lunch, I decided to take a little drive out to where I'd been the night before to see if there was anything I'd missed. And then I'd swing by the Hunts' house and take a look around there.

The Barefoot Bar and Grille was open, but there were very few customers inside. I spoke to a waitress who told me that the majority of their business was late afternoon and early evening. The only reason they stayed open for lunch was because some of the local customers and fishermen depended on them. Nothing looked suspicious there.

I left there and headed to the row of beach houses where the Hunts lived. Most of the homes were on stilts and were either painted pastel colors or were left in their natural state of rustic wood. It was really very pretty, I had to admit, and I wouldn't have minded living there. The only problem was the vulnerability to hurricanes, but I supposed I could get used to having to evacuate once every couple of years in exchange for the view they had of the Gulf of Mexico. It was breathtaking.

When I arrived, I spotted a car parked in the driveway, although there was a garage. The car looked familiar. It was a bright red sports car with a spoiler on the back. Where had I seen this car?

I parked on the street and walked up to the front of the house, having no idea what I was looking for. A sound to my right startled me, making me jump. Then, there I was, face to face with Tom Masterson. No wonder the red sports car looked familiar; it was his. I'd seen it in the parking lot at the clubhouse.

"What are you doing here, Miss Walsh?" he asked.

I raised my eyebrows and glared at him. On the surface, he looked aggressive and demanding, almost protective. But my police training had taught me to look a little deeper and study the eyes and mannerisms. I saw a subtle defensiveness that he was trying hard to cover up.

"I can ask you the same question," I stated.

"I'm looking for Barney," Tom said. "Have you seen him?"

"Why, no," I replied in the lightest tone I could manage. "I'm here looking for Alice." I was testing him to see what he knew.

His face suddenly turned white as a sheet. It was almost like he'd been caught in the act of something, but I wasn't sure what it was.

"Have you seen her?" I asked, placing my hand on my hip, tilting my head to one side to get a different perspective on this man who made the hair on the back of my neck stand on end.

He slowly shook his head. "Uh, she's not here, either."

I sighed and held my hands up in frustration. "We had a dinner meeting last night, and she didn't show up. I was worried about her, so I decided to come out and check on her."

Tom looked at me like he wasn't sure what to think; but he didn't say anything. I could tell he knew something. What I wasn't sure of was what he was doing out here.

"Do you live around here?" I asked.

"No," he replied. "I have a place on the mainland."

"Have you known Barney Hunt long?"

He narrowed his eyes. "Long enough. Why?"

"Just wondering," I replied. "How about Alice? Know anything about her?"

"Look, lady, I don't know what you're doing, but I don't like it."

"I'm not looking for your approval, Mr. Masterson. Especially now."

I watched his face change expression. He was clearly in distress over something, and I really didn't care. Maybe he couldn't find whatever it was he was looking for. I had to be careful not to spook him, or I might never get what I needed. Too bad I didn't know what that was yet.

Tom left before I did, allowing me to snoop around a little without interruption. I had no idea what I was looking for, so I checked out everything, including the garage that wasn't closed all the way.

After a quick glance over my shoulder to make sure no one was watching, I raised the garage door enough for me to get inside. Once I was in, I lowered it back to where it was.

I had to grope around in the dark to find a light switch, but once I found it and flipped it on, I had to turn it back off. It was so bright I was afraid I'd alert the neighbors.

It took me a few minutes to check for a security

alarm system. Since I'd been in law enforcement for so long, I knew exactly what to look for. It surprised me that there was none.

The door to the house from the garage wasn't locked, another fact that surprised me. People around here certainly seemed careless, but who was I to complain? It certainly made my job easier.

I knew that what I was doing was illegal, but I needed to get an edge on this case. If I'd still been a cop, I never would have gone inside, but I was a civilian now. My punishment for getting caught would be small, since I had no intention of stealing anything. I was just snooping around. Besides, I knew the captain of the night shift, so I had a feeling he would be extra lenient.

Everything in the house looked gaudy but expensive. Definitely not my taste, which was pretty simple.

The house wasn't as big as it appeared from the outside, but it had that magnificent view and lots of exposed beams and glass throughout the place. I could only imagine how expensive this house was to maintain.

I carefully and methodically moved from room to room, looking for anything that would give me a clue about the Bonita Landry case. Since Barney had already admitted to killing his wife, I figured that one was cut and dry. And I had no doubt it had been an accident, although any guy who'd beat his wife was a sleazeball in my mind.

The downstairs consisted mostly of a huge room, a kitchen, and a half bath. I had to take a spiral staircase to the second floor, which had an open loft and two bedrooms, no hallway. Everything was wide open.

All I saw in the bedrooms was the usual: beds, dressers, nightstands, and a few knickknacks. It wasn't until I headed back toward the staircase that I spotted a rolltop desk.

As I tugged at the knobs, I realized it was locked, which surprised me. Everything else around here was wide open.

The lock was pretty typical of this type of furniture—easy to pick. I used the end of a wire hanger I'd found in a closet to get into it.

What I found were things you'd normally see in a desk: bank statements, canceled checks, a few pieces of correspondence. Nothing that triggered any alarms. I was disappointed.

With a sigh, I decided to look in the master bedroom one more time. I moved a little more quickly now, since I'd already taken a long, slow look around. I hated coming up empty-handed.

This time, though, I decided to rummage through a few drawers, in the dresser and the nightstands. And that was when I found something of extreme interest in my uncle's case.

There was nothing in the dresser, with the exception of underwear, t-shirts, and shorts. It was obvious which side belonged to Alice and which side was Barney's. So I went on a hunch and figured that they slept on the same side of the bed as they claimed in their dresser.

Barney's nightstand was filled with a flashlight, a

pocket knife, and a few odds and ends. Nothing unusual.

But Alice's nightstand held one of the most valuable pieces of evidence I'd found since I'd been looking. There, lying on top of a pack of stationery, was something that totally shocked me. One of Uncle Bing's monogrammed handkerchiefs! What was she doing with that?

Carefully closing the nightstand drawer, I just stood there and contemplated what I should do next. Had the cops looked around here yet? Did they know about the handkerchief? I wanted to ask Uncle Bing about it, but how could I without letting him know I'd walked into the Hunts' house uninvited? I was in a bind, and I knew it. This would take considerable thought and calculation to get someone to take a look at this.

As quickly as I could, I made my way back to the garage, taking extra precautions to leave everything as I'd found it. I'd been very careful not to leave fingerprints by using my sleeve to touch knobs and furniture. The only place where my fingers had touched was the dresser, and I'd wiped the surface until it shone. It was highly unlikely anyone would find my fingerprints in this house.

Now that I knew my uncle's handkerchief was in Alice's nightstand, I had to think that Ms. Landry's killer might have been her daughter. After all, if Alice had managed to get ahold of one of his hankies, she probably could have gotten more. I needed to ask Uncle Bing, but how could I do it without letting on where I'd been?

My mind raced as I drove back to Gulfside Country Club. All sorts of things flitted through my brain, but nothing seemed logical. Why would Alice have wanted to kill her mother? There was no money for inheritance, and they somehow managed to avoid each other, with the exception of an occasional brief visit, even though they both lived in the same small town. Sure, they talked on the phone and even argued a lot, but that was harmless. No one ever died from a phone conversation.

I parked my car in the spot closest to the building, then hopped out and went to see Uncle Bing. He didn't seem to have anything better to do than greet me when I came back from wherever I went. "Hi, Summer. Anything new?"

I shook my head. This was a very touchy issue, and I knew I'd have to handle it with kid gloves.

"Uncle Bing, would you mind if we had a long talk?" I finally said when we were inside with the door closed.

"Sure, Summer," he said with a note of concern in his voice. "But if it's about Bonita, I promise you I didn't do it."

"I know. You've already told me. But I want to talk about your relationship with her. What did the two of you do when you went out?"

His face turned bright red. My uncle, the man-about-town, actually blushed. If the situation hadn't been so serious, I would have smiled.

"We went out to eat, or I cooked." He chuckled as he remembered something. "Bonita didn't like to cook, and that's good because she managed to mess up boiling water."

"What else?" I asked. I had to know everything to get the clues I needed. Even if I had to guide him to lead me to the correct answer.

"She loved to go to the movies, especially the tear-jerkers."

I'd gotten him where I wanted him faster than I thought I would. "And that's how she got your hand-kerchief, right?"

He nodded. "That's right." I watched him cross his legs, fold his arms, and look down. He wasn't aware of the fact that he was closing himself off to me, but I didn't mind. I'd still manage to get him to open up.

"Did you give her more than one?"

"Of course," he said. "I was taught to be a gentle-man. But she always laundered them and gave them back." He gulped. "Except for the one that was on her when they found her body."

I sucked in a breath and went on. "Did you ever hand them out to anyone else?"

Slowly shaking his head, he looked thoughtful for a moment. "Not that I can think of." He narrowed his eyes, then raised his eyebrows as if he'd just remem-bered something. "Wait a minute! I did hand her granddaughter one last time she came to visit. We were on a picnic, and she spilled soda all over the front of her blouse. I gave her my handkerchief, and she said she'd send it back to me."

"Did you ever get it back?" I asked.

"Not that I remember," he said after a more thoughtful moment. "But I really never expected to. Why?"

"I don't know," I said, turning to avoid his gaze. "I just wondered."

Uncle Bing stood from where he'd been sitting in the living room and walked toward his bedroom. Then, he turned and smiled at me. "You're working so hard for me, Summer, and I appreciate it. Just don't give yourself an ulcer over it."

I grinned back at him before he turned back and went to his room. There had to be something I could do to get to the bottom of this. That was when I decided to call Captain Stokes. Jerry.

The rest of that afternoon I watched the clock so I could catch him at the beginning of his shift. Then I gave him fifteen minutes to get his coffee and get situated at his desk before I placed the call.

He was on the phone within seconds of when I was put on hold. His voice held affection that made me feel guilty, since I was having to manipulate him to get to the evidence in Alice's nightstand drawer.

"Jerry, has anyone from the police department searched the Hunts' house?" I asked.

"Of course we have," he replied. "Why?"

"Just wondering." I glanced down at my hands and inspected my nails while trying to think of what to say next. Finally, I sucked in a breath and then let it out while I said, "Anything suspicious?"

"What do you mean, Summer?" he asked.

"You know. Anything to tie either Barney or Alice to Ms. Landry's murder?"

"Do you know something?"

"Well," I began, hesitating for a few seconds. "It does seem strange that there were no murders in Gulf-side for years, and now there are two so close together. And the fact that they're mother and daughter makes it doubly suspicious."

"Yes," he said. "I agree. But you sound like you might be getting at something."

"What I want to know is if you found anything when you looked through Alice's or Barney's things. Anything that might have belonged to Ms. Landry or shown a motive we might not have thought of."

"Do you know something you're not telling me?" he asked.

I felt my blood pressure rise. I hated lying, but I couldn't very well tell him I'd let myself into the Hunts' house. "I have a hunch that we're missing something," I said.

"Would you like for us to look again?"

"Yes." There. That was easy enough.

"Is there anything else, Summer?"

"Um," I began, trying to think of a way to put what I wanted him to do. Then, I decided to use the direct approach. "Would you mind being there during the investigation?"

"Me?" he asked. "Personally?"

"Yes, you, in person. I want to make sure no stone is left unturned."

"How would you like to accompany me, then?" he asked.

That was the best thing he could have asked. I'd be there, and I could somehow guide the investigators right to the nightstand. "You bet!" I said.

He chuckled. "How did I know you'd say yes?"

"Because you're a good cop?"

"Uh huh," was his only response.

I chatted for a few minutes about what we needed to look for, while he listened. Finally, he said, "Can you meet me there in about two hours? I'll have to put in the paperwork to get this thing going again."

"I'll be there," I agreed.

I was amazed at how quickly he was able to get things done. But who was I to argue?

When I met Jerry at the Hunts' house, several other cops were standing outside talking to a neighbor. I joined them.

"Some guy was here about an hour ago. When I asked him what he was doing snooping around, he said he was Alice's son-in-law, so I figured it was okay for him to go inside."

Chapter Twelve

I gulped. "Alice's son-in-law was here? I thought he lived in Mississippi. What's he like?" I'd been wondering where Bonita's granddaughter was.

He nodded. "Kind of a nervous fellow, if you ask me, but he seemed okay."

"Did he say what he wanted?" I asked.

"No, he just said he had a few things he wanted to take a look at. And since they never locked their place, I didn't think there was anything in there of any value, so it was okay. Most people lock up valuable possessions, anyway."

My heart sank. What if the son-in-law had done something to botch the investigation?

The man finally backed off, and we went inside, very careful not to touch anything that would leave fingerprints. It took every ounce of self-restraint to keep from telling everyone where to go and what drawers to open, and that they needed to look in the nightstand in the master bedroom. But I was on my best behavior. I stood to the side while they inspected the contents in every single drawer in the kitchen, then looked beneath sofa cushions and behind the few doors on that floor. I even directed them to some places where I knew they wouldn't find anything so when I made sure they looked in the right drawer, they wouldn't suspect I already knew something.

Finally, it was time to head upstairs. My pulse raced as I followed the team.

We went to the master bedroom first. Good. Maybe I could lead them to the nightstand and then my heart would slow down to a manageable rate.

What we saw when we got up there was nothing like what I'd seen earlier. There must have been a half dozen things that had been added to the room, all things related to murder. My face grew hot with anger and frustration.

"Look at this, will ya?" one of the investigators said. "None of this stuff was here earlier."

So they *had* been there. Surely, they would know someone had tampered with the evidence.

"Did you take pictures?" I asked.

One of the younger cops nodded. "We *always* take pictures."

At least they had that, I figured. But what weight would the handkerchief in the nightstand carry now?

I nodded to the dresser. "Have you checked the contents of the drawers?"

"We opened them, but we didn't remove anything."

"All the drawers?" I asked.

He pointed to the dresser. "We looked in the obvious places, like the dresser."

"How about the rest of the furniture?" I asked, hoping I wouldn't sound too obvious.

Jerry squinted at me. "Do you know something we should know, Summer?"

I felt my frustration growing by the minute. "I just want to do whatever I can to help my uncle. He's still a suspect, isn't he?"

"Yes," Jerry admitted. He turned to the other members of the team and told them to open all the drawers and do a thorough search. They complied.

It took them nearly ten minutes to get to the nightstands. When the cop who was on Alice's side of the bed opened her drawer, I was right there. He started to close it after rummaging through it, and I wanted to stop him. But I didn't have to.

"Wait a minute," Jerry said as he came over there. "What's this?"

He pointed his flashlight at the handkerchief lying on top. He lifted it and stuck it inside a plastic bag. Then, something else caught our eye. It was a snapshot that had been lying beneath it. We all got closer.

The picture was taken at some big function—it looked like it might have been at a picnic—and my uncle was in it. He had his arms around a woman who looked like other pictures I'd seen of Bonita Landry and a younger woman who resembled her. It must have been Ms. Landry's granddaughter; I knew it wasn't Alice.

"Well, well, well," Jerry said as he lifted it carefully from the drawer. "I wonder what Alice Hunt was doing with this."

I swallowed hard. I'd heard that Alice was semi-estranged from both her mother and her daughter since marrying Barney. Why was that picture in the drawer?

"That is rather odd," I said softly. Jerry also knew about the relationship-gone-bad. "Maybe she kept the picture there so she could look at them when she got lonely."

"Looks like we need to get back to work," Jerry finally said after we stood there and stared at the picture for a few more minutes. "We have more questions to ask, and we need to find out what Mrs. Hunt's son-in-law was doing here."

The first thing Jerry wanted to do was go back to see my uncle. "I think there are some things he's not telling us," he said softly. "But I don't want you with me while I talk to him."

"And why not?" I barked.

"See? You're too much on edge. You're too close to your uncle. There are some answers we need to know, and I can't have you interrupting and getting upset when I ask the questions that are necessary to get to the bottom of it."

After cooling off for a few seconds, I finally said, "Okay, but let me talk to him right after you're finished."

"No problem," he said with a smile. "It shouldn't take too long."

We got back to Uncle Bing's condo, where we spotted two unmarked police cars. Jerry frowned.

"What are they doing here?" he asked.

"More investigation, I suppose."

"I wasn't informed of anything happening here today."

Jerry was out of the car in two seconds flat. He turned to me and said, "Stay right here. I'll come back and get you."

I nodded. I had a bad feeling about this, but I knew better than to interfere.

It took Jerry approximately five minutes before he came walking out of the condo with Uncle Bing, two police officers following close behind them. Neither my uncle nor Jerry looked too pleased with how things had gone. As they walked right past me, I had to do a double-take. My uncle's hands were behind his back, and held together by handcuffs. Jerry had arrested Uncle Bing again.

"What's going on?" I shrieked.

Jerry just shook his head and walked my uncle to his car, where he helped him into the back seat. I called after him, but after looking at me for a second, he turned and got back behind the wheel of his car.

I quickly hopped back into my own car and followed them all the way to the police station. This was getting ridiculous, the way they were treating my uncle.

The desk sergeant managed to keep me from running down the hall after Jerry and Uncle Bing until Jerry came back. "Come on, Summer. We need to talk."

He gently took my arm, but I yanked it away. "Get your hands off me," I growled.

"Suit yourself. C'mon."

We went into his office and he closed the door behind him. Then, he gestured toward the chair and instructed me to have a seat.

"I'd prefer to stand," I hissed.

"Okay. As long as you keep your mouth shut and listen to me," he said, this time throwing his authority in my face. "I had to arrest your uncle."

"Why? You know he didn't kill anyone."

"I don't know any such thing at this point," Jerry admitted. "It doesn't look good for him at all. Seems your uncle decided to take matters in his own hands and inspect Bonita's condo."

"When?"

Jerry sucked in a breath and slowly let it out, making me wait for an answer. "Seems Delta and her ex are back from their trip. They spotted your uncle letting himself into Bonita's apartment, and they called the cops."

"Where was Uncle Bing when you found him?" I asked. "Did you catch him in the act?"

"Didn't have to," he replied. "When I asked him where he'd been earlier, he told me."

"What did he say?" I asked.

"Seems the granddaughter and her husband weren't too happy about your uncle being on Ms. Landry's bank accounts, so they confronted him. He stood up to the son-in-law and said that Bonita could do whatever she pleased with her money, and if she chose to add him to the account, that was her business."

Shaking my head, I looked at Jerry like he'd lost his mind. "But that doesn't implicate him."

"No, it doesn't, but breaking and entering is a serious offense."

"How did he break in?" I asked.

Jerry shook his head. "He has a key."

"So, that's not exactly breaking and entering. Apparently, lots of people have the key to Ms. Landry's condo."

"But they're not all suspects in her murder," Jerry reminded me.

Granted, he was right. But still, I didn't think he should arrest Uncle Bing if he didn't follow up on everyone else who had the key.

"Apparently, your uncle is also making wild threats."

"Threats?" I asked.

Jerry took a step back as if he thought I might do something. "We've heard from several sources that he made all kinds of threats to protect Ms. Landry. He told me himself he threatened them and told them to leave Ms. Landry alone."

"What did he threaten to do?" I asked as I sank down in the chair behind me. My mother had always told me how Uncle Bing liked to sound more important than he was. But he was harmless, wasn't he? At least I'd never seen the violent side of him.

"He told Ms. Landry's daughter that he'd kill to protect what didn't belong to them in the first place."

"Uncle Bing told you that?"

Jerry nodded. I could see he was telling the truth. Besides, what good would it do for him to lie to me? He had nothing to gain.

"You don't think he killed Ms. Landry, do you?" I asked. I knew now that the course of the investigation would change, with Uncle Bing in custody again.

Shaking his head, he replied, "At this point, I don't know what to think." He cleared his throat. "But no, I still don't believe your uncle did it."

To be honest, I didn't know what to think, either. Right when I thought I was heading up the right track, someone derailed me. In all the time I'd been a detective, nothing this bizarre had ever happened. Why did it have to happen to Uncle Bing?

"That's not all, Summer," he went on. "We found a letter written to Alice and Barney Hunt that sounded an awful lot like he would do anything to keep the money in his name and out of Alice's daughter's."

"You did?" I kept on hearing surprises. Uncle Bing had never been the greedy type with money. He was more concerned about the ladies.

Nodding, Jerry added, "Before, when he was released, the day shift captain said that the handkerchief could have gotten into the wrong person's hands and that we really didn't have enough to detain John, er Bing. But now we have so much evidence weighted against him that we can't possibly let him go."

"You don't really think there's enough evidence

against Uncle Bing, do you?" I asked, hoping he'd be totally honest with me, now that we were friends. It seemed like he was the only one who wasn't guarded when I was around.

"Not really, but I do think it's a good idea to keep him locked up, if nothing else but for his protection."

I saw his point, but I didn't agree. And the irony of the whole thing was that Uncle Bing and Barney Hunt were next door neighbors in their jail cells. Two of the most unlikely men to ever get together.

"I want to see my uncle," I finally said, barely above a whisper. "He's probably fit to be tied."

"Actually," Jerry said, "he's taking this quite well. I think he's relieved to be out of the way."

"You've got to be kidding," I retorted as I followed Jerry down the long hallway I was growing increasingly familiar with.

I only had to wait a minute before Uncle Bing was sitting across the table from me. He leaned over it and winked. "We've got to quit meeting like this. Your mother won't like it a bit."

"No," I agreed, "she won't. But she doesn't need to know about this until it's all over."

"Uh, Summer," he said. "It's too late for that. I called her when I first arrived and told her you might need her support."

I groaned. My mom had always hated the fact that I was into police work. And now that I was out of it, I had a feeling she'd do whatever it took to keep me out. No matter who needed my help.

"When will she be here?" I asked.

"She's not coming," he replied, looking down at the table.

"She's not?" I screeched. In spite of my earlier thoughts, I was shocked. How dare my mom not come to show her brother support at a time like this?

"No, she said she didn't want to upset you when you were so obviously bent on crawling right back into the cops and robbers game you seem to enjoy so much."

I had to bite my lip again because of the smile that kept threatening to cross my face. While I had mixed feelings about my mother coming, it was really best that she stayed away. I had work to do, and I wasn't in the mood to entertain.

"Okay, Uncle Bing, I don't have long," I finally said as I decided to get back to the business at hand. "We need to get your attorney to start working on this."

"Don't have one," he said.

"What?"

"I don't have an attorney."

"But I thought—"

"I never told you I had an attorney. You mentioned it once, but I never said you were right. I figured that you'd leave me alone about it if I didn't tell you. I don't feel like I need to spend all my money just to prove I'm innocent. Attorneys are for guilty people."

I blew out another exasperated breath. Uncle Bing could really try a sane person with his cockamamie thoughts on how things were done. "Trust me, Uncle Bing, you need a criminal attorney. And the best one we can get."

"You're starting to sound like that Captain Stokes fella. Do all cops think alike?"

"No," I replied. "It's just that cops see how important it is to have a good attorney when you're accused of first degree murder."

"But I didn't do it, Summer," he said. "How many times do I hafta tell ya?"

"That's all the more reason you need an attorney. To prove your innocence."

"You're not making sense, Summer, but if you feel like I need an attorney, why don't you find me one?"

I nodded. "Okay, I'll do that as soon as I leave here. But in the meantime I need to know a few things."

"Okay, shoot."

I asked question after question about what he knew of Bonita Landry's granddaughter and her husband. He told me of the times he'd met them, plus he gave me his impression.

"The granddaughter is okay, but sort of a weak young woman. That husband of hers sort of reminds me a little of Barney. He's a greedy little fella. Wants money that isn't his. I think he might have married for money and been sorely disappointed."

I'd heard that story before. It happened all the time. If people were marrying for money, I figured they needed to do an audit before they said their final vows.

"Do you think they'd kill for money?" I asked.

He shrugged. "I never thought of it before, but I suppose anything's possible."

"How can I get in touch with them?" I asked.

Uncle Bing drummed his fingers on the table as he

looked up to the ceiling. Then, his face lit up. "Bonita handed me a slip of paper with their address on it, and seems I remember sticking it in my address book."

"Where's your address book?" I asked.

"It's that little black book on the telephone table, in the drawer where I keep my reading glasses."

I'd seen his book that was even labeled *Little Black Book*. When I spotted it, I thought it was cute that someone Uncle Bing's age would have such a thing. But now cute wasn't what I was thinking.

Chapter Thirteen

"This is the granddaughter named Tiffany, right?"
I asked as I backed toward the door.

"That's right," he replied. "But I can't for the life
of me remember her last name."

"Do you know her husband's real name?"

"Shark."

"His real name is Shark?" I said, scrunching up my
nose. "I don't think that's right. Do you have any other
names for him?"

With a quick shake of his head and a smirk, he
replied, "I was introduced to them as Tiffany and
Shark. That's all anyone called him the whole time
they visited Bonita."

"And you don't remember their last name?"

"No, I can't recall ever hearing it."

"Does this little slip of paper I'm looking for say 'Tiffany and Shark'?"

He nodded. "I believe that's all it says. Oh, it might have their address on it, too." He narrowed his eyes as he jogged his memory. "Yeah, that's right. It has their phone number and address."

At least that would help, I thought. Hopefully, that slip of paper was still in his *Little Black Book.*

I rushed back to Uncle Bing's condo and pulled open the drawer of the phone stand. The book was lying right on top of everything else. I carefully opened it and flipped through the pages to find a slip of paper with "Tiffany and Shark's" address and phone number. It was stuck right smack dab in the middle of the book.

With a shaky and anxious finger, I punched in the phone number that was on the paper. A squeaky little girl's voice came on the line.

"Hello?" she said, a huge question lingering long after she answered. When I didn't say anything, she repeated, "Hello?"

"Uh, this is Summer Walsh calling from Florida. May I please speak to Tiffany?" I hadn't heard about Tiffany having children.

"Speaking," she said.

No, couldn't be, I thought. I must have misunderstood. "I'm looking for Tiffany who's married to Shark, daughter of Alice Hunt, granddaughter of Bonita Landry."

She giggled in that little girl's voice and said, "This is Tiffany. The one you're looking for."

Surely, she wouldn't be giggling if she'd just lost a mother and grandmother to the hands of murderers within a week of each other. But maybe she would. I didn't know this young woman.

"Has anyone contacted you about your mother, Tiffany?" I asked, trying for an authoritative voice.

Suddenly, there was a chill over the phone line. Her voice deepened, almost to the level of most adults. "My mother and I haven't spoken in a while."

"Oh," I said. And they wouldn't ever speak again. I wondered if she knew that. "When was the last time you talked to your grandmother?"

"Uh, let's see," she said. There was a moment of silence before she said, "Who did you say this was again?"

"Summer Walsh. John Smith's niece."

"I'm sorry, but I don't know John Smith," she said.

"You might know him as Bing." I hadn't been sure what Ms. Landry had introduced him as.

"Oh, yes, how is he? Are he and my grandmother still hot and heavy?" she asked in that little girl's voice again.

"N-no," I stuttered. So she didn't have any idea about either her mother or her grandmother. Talk about a dysfunctional family. Then, I got a brilliant idea. "Why don't you take a little trip down here? I'd like to talk to you."

"I'm sorry, but my husband is out of town, and I don't go anywhere without him," she said. "But maybe we can take a weekend trip next month."

I didn't want to tell her the news over the phone,

but I didn't see where I had any choice now. She needed to know, and obviously the local authorities were too caught up in the moment to call the next of kin. Jerry had given me the impression she'd been notified, but come to think of it, no one had come out and said that was the case.

The news of her mother's death didn't seem to faze her, but it took me almost a half hour to calm her down over the loss of her grandmother. Apparently, Bonita Landry had been the only person in her family who'd shown her love. And from where I sat, it appeared that the only two people who truly loved the deceased elderly woman were her granddaughter and my Uncle Bing. I was almost certain that neither of them would have murdered her. The one I needed to talk to now was Shark.

"Tiffany, honey," I said, using a term of endearment I'd never used with anyone in my life. "Is there another name for your husband besides 'Shark'?"

"Yes," she replied. "His real name is Gomer."

"Gomer?" I asked, having to stifle a laugh. "And your last name?"

"Heath," she replied.

No wonder he went by "Shark." What were his parents thinking when they named him?

"Any idea where your husband is, Tiffany?" I asked. I wasn't sure if she knew he'd come to Florida or if she thought he was on some secret mission with the military.

"He went on a fishing trip with some of the other

enlisted guys from the base," she replied. "They do this once in a while. Helps them unwind."

What was it about men telling their wives they were going off on trips with the guys when they were somewhere else? Looked to me like Alice's daughter followed in her footsteps when it came to choosing men.

"Okay, Tiffany, thanks. I hope you don't mind if I call you back later. Will Gomer . . . I mean Shark be home Monday?"

"He should be," she replied with a sniffle.

After I hung up, I had the feeling I might be on to something. Last time I heard about a guy lying to his wife about his whereabouts, he turned out to be a murderer. And that was Barney.

There were a few people who'd suggested that Barney might have killed Ms. Landry. Even Uncle Bing thought that was a possibility. But something else was bothering me. I'd been driving by the tennis courts at least three or four times a day since I'd been in Gulfside, and I hadn't seen any activity around the tennis courts in the past couple of days, with the exception of Delta and her ex-husband, Henry. They looked like they were having the time of their lives.

The hair on the back of my neck stood on end. This was a sign that I was getting close to figuring out who'd killed Bonita Landry. But for the first time since I'd been trained as a detective, I had no idea which clues to follow. There were so many little things, so many hints. However, they all led in different directions. Even Alice, although she was dead, was a possibility. She and her mother had disliked each other so much, she could have done it.

I also had the feeling that Jerry didn't really think my uncle was a murderer. I didn't think he was just telling me that to throw me off course. He was too relaxed around Uncle Bing to be suspicious. I'd been around enough cops to know what we acted like when we were with cold-blooded murderers. No, Jerry didn't consider Uncle Bing a suspect; of that, I was fairly certain.

Whatever the case, I needed to find Tom Masterson. My gut instincts told me I should talk to him; I might find something that would lead me to solve the puzzle.

The first thing I tried was calling the tennis pro shop. Some young man answered, his voice cracking like a teenager's. "No, he's not here. Hasn't been for a few days," he said.

"Do you know when he'll be back?" I asked.

"I'm not sure. He's not on the schedule at all this week."

So who was giving tennis lessons to the lovely people at Gulfside Country Club? Wasn't that one of the reasons people moved here?

"Do you want me to give him a message when he returns?" the boy asked.

"N-no, thanks," I replied. "I'll try his apartment."

I started to dial his number but hung up halfway through. This would be better in person, I thought. I was generally pretty good at reading people's faces.

Since I wasn't sure what I'd be facing, I waited and called Jerry and asked him if he'd go with me. "Sure,

Summer," he said. "I was thinking of doing the same thing."

That night, he picked me up from the parking lot of Uncle Bing's condo. "I think we might be getting close," he said. "Several things came in to the police station today, and I want you to take a look at them."

"Like what?" I asked, trying to hide the fact that I was pleased Jerry was including me on this case.

"Information on Bonita's granddaughter and husband. Apparently, Gomer Heath is under investigation for some petty crimes on the base where he's stationed. The military doesn't cut much slack for anything out of line, including stealing change from the petty cash fund."

I raised my eyebrows. "He's in trouble for that?"

"Yes," he replied, "that among several other things."

Shaking my head in astonishment, I said, "Some people can be so stupid."

"I know, and that's why you and I are in law enforcement."

"You seem to forget a very important thing, Jerry," I said softly.

"What's that?"

"I *was* in law enforcement. I'm not now."

He chuckled softly. "Coulda fooled me."

When we arrived at Tom's apartment complex, I found myself looking around, nervous about what we might encounter. I had an uneasy feeling about things, like danger might be lurking around the next corner.

"Ready?" Jerry asked as he patted his hip, casually checking to make sure he had packed his gun.

With a quick nod, I said, "Let's go."

I knocked on the door, but Jerry was right by my side. I'd halfway expected *not* to see Tom, since his car wasn't in the parking lot. But he answered within a minute of when we got there. And he wasn't happy at all to see us.

"Whaddya want?" he asked gruffly. "I'm on vacation."

Jerry stepped forward and flashed his badge. "We'd like to have a chat with you, Masterson."

Tom rolled his eyes. "I know who you are," he said. "Come in and do what you have to do. Just don't take too long."

There was a young man sitting at the kitchen table when we went inside. He looked up but quickly glanced back down at his coffee. No one bothered to introduce him. I had a feeling we needed to know who he was.

Jerry was the one to step up to the table and start asking questions. "Captain Jerry Stokes with the Gulfside Police Department."

The man nodded and looked back at the table. Tom stood there glaring at Jerry. The silence thundered and echoed through the kitchen until it felt like it might explode.

Finally, I sucked in a breath and said, "Just tell us who you are. The suspense is killing me."

The young man glanced over his shoulder at Tom. Tom nodded and spoke for him. "This is Shark."

My ears perked up. Shark! Bingo! We were on to something; I could feel it in my bones.

Jerry cast a quick glance my way. He knew it, too. Then he turned back around and faced the man still sitting there, staring at some spot on the table.

"I thought you were in Mississippi, fishing with some buddies," he said.

The look of surprise on Shark's face was worth all the clues in the world. "Who told you—?"

"Never mind," Jerry said, acting quickly and grabbing him by the arm. "I've been in touch with the U.S. Air Force, and I've promised them that if you ever show your face in this neck of the woods, I'll let them know. You're coming with me."

"Wait a minute," Tom said, trying to intervene, but unsuccessfully. "You can't do that. He's my house-guest."

"You should have warned him that the Gulfside cops don't like fugitives in our town. It dirties up the place," Jerry growled.

I wasn't quite sure what was going on, but I played along with Jerry. He seemed to know what he was doing, and he was doing a good job.

We managed to get Shark handcuffed and into the car. Jerry suggested I stay behind with Mr. Masterson while he brought Gomer Heath back to the police station.

"I hope we don't have anyone else we have to lock up," he whispered, as he slammed the car door shut. "We only have three jail cells, and after I put Gomer here in one of them, there will be no more vacancies."

Before he went around to his side, he added, "Now that Shark's out of the way, get as much information out of Masterson as you can."

"You can always let Uncle Bing go if you're too crowded." I thought I'd take advantage of the opportunity to say something, knowing that it wouldn't do a bit of good. He just looked at me, said, "Just talk to Masterson, will ya?" then went about his business of hauling Shark back to the station.

I have to admit, I was a little afraid of being alone with Tom Masterson; he gave me the creeps. I didn't have a gun with me, since I'd made the decision to give up law enforcement. Maybe I'd have to rethink the gun issue. It sure did give me peace of mind during situations like this.

Fortunately, Tom didn't resist when I wanted back into his apartment. In fact, he even offered me something to drink. I turned him down.

Once I sat down, he stood and stared at me for a long time before he said, "I didn't kill anyone, you know."

I raised my eyebrows but didn't say anything. Listening was what I needed to do right now.

He went on. "I never did like the old broad. She got on my nerves something fierce with that whiny little voice and always asking for credit. But I didn't kill her."

I continued to sit there and stare at him, nodding and acknowledging that I was listening. Tom licked his lips and cleared his throat. I glanced down at the carpet that needed steam cleaning.

"And Shark didn't do it, either."

My head snapped up, and my heart nearly stopped. It sounded like he was getting awfully close to telling me something important, and I needed to give him my full attention.

"When Henry came to us and offered us money to get rid of your uncle, we had to laugh at him," Tom said. "I have no idea where he came up with the notion that we were involved in something like that."

"Henry?" I asked in a squeaky voice. "Delta's ex-husband. Are you saying that Henry killed Bonita Landry?"

He started to nod, but then he thought better of it. "Can't say for sure, but he wanted your uncle out of the way."

"That doesn't mean he killed Ms. Landry, though," I said. But it sure did make him a serious suspect, I thought.

"No, it doesn't," Tom said, looking at me as if I were crazy or stupid. "But I think it's strong enough evidence to convict him of something."

Just then a crazy thought of the crowded Gulfside jail went through my mind. Someone had to be let go, and I wondered who that would be.

"Did he offer you and Gomer—I mean Shark— money to kill Uncle Bing?" I asked.

"Yes, money and a condo at Gulfside Country Club," he replied, offering much more information than I ever thought I'd get from him.

"Are you willing to testify to this in court?" I asked.

He inhaled through his large nostrils, then let it out

as he shut his eyes and nodded. "Yes, I will. I don't see where I have any choice at this point."

"What's your connection with Shark?" I asked.

"That," he said firmly, "is none of your business."

I had a feeling I'd find out soon enough, so I just nodded and went on to the next subject. "Any idea where Henry is right now?" I asked. "He went away on vacation for a while, and I've only seen him a couple times after he got back." Come to think of it, I hadn't seen him for the past couple of days, which was unusual.

"He's home," Tom replied, "keeping a low profile. I spoke with him this morning when he called."

"What did he want?"

"You don't want to know," he said, as he backed away from me.

"Oh, yes, I do." Standing up, I quickly walked over to Tom and literally backed him into a corner.

I could tell he was nervous. "He wants you out of the picture too," he said flatly.

My blood ran cold. I never expected such an exciting vacation in Gulfside, first almost getting run into the Gulf of Mexico by Barney Hunt, and then a squeaky little bald guy named Henry wanting to have me killed.

"What did you tell him?" I asked.

"I told the old man he was crazy."

Then something began to bother me about all this. "I've got a question, Tom."

"What?" he asked as he picked up a stress ball and began to squeeze.

"Why would Henry come to you if he wanted someone killed? Does he know something about you that we need to know?"

Tom started to shake his head, then thought better of it. "When Clyde got Crestview Country Club Communities to hire me, he was told to check my background. He got Henry to do it. I got in a little trouble a few years ago, so I paid him to keep his mouth shut about it. I really needed this job."

"So he held it over your head the whole time, getting you to do things he wasn't willing to do," I added.

"I did most of them too, but I refuse to kill people." I believed him.

"And Shark?" I asked.

Tom shrugged. "We met back when I was in the military. In fact, I introduced him to Ms. Landry's granddaughter. She's a real beauty."

It sure is a small world, I thought. I wondered what else Tom had done to get on Ms. Landry's bad side.

"I need to use the phone, Tom," I said. "Where is it?"

He pointed to the living room. "In there. You'd better not waste any time getting over to the condos. Clyde is starting to get nervous."

With shaky fingers, I dialed Jerry's cell phone number. He answered right away. I told him to meet me in the condo parking lot. He told me to keep Tom Masterson by my side. I groaned.

Finally, when I got off the phone, I looked at Tom and said, "Put a shirt on. You're coming with me."

He started to say no, but then he nodded. "It'll take me just a minute."

I followed him into his bedroom, holding my breath the whole time. I couldn't let him see how nervous I was. "You're not leaving my sight, Tom. I'm sure you understand that."

Fortunately, he didn't resist anything I told him to do. We went to the parking lot, where he led me to a car I'd never seen before. "It's a rental. My car's in the shop."

Just as we got to the condo parking lot, Clyde Bullhouser was heading out. I jumped out of Tom's car and hollered, "Stop, Mr. Bullhouser! We need to talk."

Mr. Bullhouser glared at me. I wondered what had made him so mad. "I don't have time," he said.

"There's something you need to know," I yelled back to make sure he could hear me.

He ignored me and got into his car, anyway. Tom stepped on the accelerator, the door of the rental car still open, and squealed away from where I still stood. *Oh, man, Jerry would be furious with me!* was my first thought. I wasn't supposed to let Tom out of my sight.

But then, he stopped at the entrance to the parking lot, blocking it. That was when I realized that Tom was trying to help me. He wasn't going to let Mr. Bullhouser out, at least not in his car.

"What was that all about?" I asked, my nerves still on the edge of my skin.

Tom shrugged. "I dunno. I just figure it's time to start helping a little. It's the least I can do."

I watched as Mr. Bullhouser wavered, trying to decide what to do next. He seemed to be having trouble. I wondered why he was choosing to ignore me.

Taking advantage of the few extra seconds of time, I ran over to him and grabbed him in a hold I'd learned as a cop. He was no match for me, in spite of his size being nearly double mine. I managed to hold him until Tom joined me and gave me a hand.

"I still have no idea why you're doing this, Tom," I said, "but thanks."

With a half smile, he said, "I'm tired of hiding and running. It's starting to get to me."

Mr. Bullhouser shuddered for a moment, pulling my guard back up. Then, he began to sob. "I loved her. Bonita was the only woman I've ever really loved. I would never kill Bonita. I didn't do it."

"I know it," I said.

Tom cast a warning glance at me, then started on something that baffled me. "Come on, Clyde," Tom said with a note of irritation. "Stop the blubbering. I told her everything."

"But I didn't do it."

What was Tom up to? I knew something was going on, so I took a step back.

"Well, then, Mr. Bullhouser," I said in my old cop voice. "Any idea who did it?"

He squeezed his eyes shut and nodded. "Delta."

My head fell forward in surprise at this turn of events. "Delta?" I said hoarsely. "Wait a minute," I said, as I tightened my grip on his shoulder. "Delta isn't exactly the strongest woman in the world. How could she have strangled Ms. Landry?"

"I don't know, but I do know that Bonita had coffee and a tennis match with her on the morning of her murder. When I asked her how the match turned out, she had a stricken look on her face. Kidding around, I told her she looked like she wanted to kill someone, and that's when she told me she and Bonita had gotten into an argument, and she'd hit her over the head with her tennis racket." Now Clyde was talking freely, and he didn't seem to want to shut up. I wasn't sure if I believed him, but I knew we needed to listen.

"Why didn't you tell us this before?" I asked.

He shook his head. "Delta isn't exactly the most stable woman in the world. No telling what she'd do to me if she knew I'd talked." His forehead crinkled. "Besides, she hit Bonita over the head. The cops said Bonita was strangled."

When the squeal of tires rounded the corner, I glanced up and saw Jerry's unmarked police car. He didn't even bother turning off the engine before he hopped out and ran over to where we were holding Mr. Bullhouser.

He yanked out the handcuffs and had Clyde Bullhouser in custody before anyone else could utter another word. "Wait a minute," I said, as he shoved his suspect into the back seat. "We need to talk."

Jerry looked at me like I was crazy, but nodded, folding his arms across his chest. Then, I told him an abbreviated version of what I'd just heard about Henry and Delta.

After mumbling something about nothing like this ever happening in Gulfside, he called for backup. "I have no idea where we're gonna put all these people."

"How about Motel 6?" I asked, trying to take some of the pressure off. He just glared at me. Then he called for an emergency warrant for Delta and Henry, just in case.

As soon as the patrol car came and took Clyde Bullhouser away and handed him the paperwork for Delta and Henry, Jerry and I went up to see the odd couple who'd managed to escape suspicion until now. I'd studied the list of where people lived in this association so long, I knew their address by heart. No one answered Henry's door when we knocked, so we headed down for Delta's place.

"I-I'm sorry, but my wife can't come to the door right now," Henry said through the three-inch crack the chain lock allowed.

"Tell her she doesn't have a choice. I have a warrant for her arrest." A look of confusion crossed Jerry's face. "Your wife? I thought the two of you were divorced."

"We just remarried on our trip," he said with a smile. Then, he became serious once again. "Just a minute," Henry said, backing away from the door. "Let me see if she's decent."

Jerry never moved his foot away from the door. We waited for a couple of minutes before I got a funny feeling again. Something was happening inside that condo, and I didn't like the possibilities that went through my mind.

"I'll be back in a minute, Jerry," I said as I began to back away. "Listen for me, and come if I call."

"Wha—?" he started but stopped as I rounded the corner to the back of the building.

Just as I'd suspected, Henry and Delta were lowering themselves to the ground from her first floor condo. Henry let out a yelp as he snagged himself on the holly bushes. Delta panicked and yanked him by the collar. I hollered for Jerry. He was there in a flash.

"Well, I'll be," he said as we watched the elderly couple struggling to escape.

"Don't forget to have forensics look into the hit over the head," I said. "And check on the autopsy report."

Jerry hung his head. "There was no autopsy report."

"What?" I shrieked.

He let out a breath and looked up at the sky. "I know, I know, I messed up. That handkerchief was so tight around her neck, we were certain her death was by strangulation."

Chapter Fourteen

With the evidence we now had, there was no doubt who'd murdered Bonita Landry. Jerry was able to scare Henry enough to get the little man to admit the fact that he'd covered for his ex-wife.

"I love her so much, I'd do anything for that woman," Henry said.

"Even lie for her?" I asked.

With a gulp that made his Adam's apple bob, he nodded. "Yes, even lie for her."

"Do you realize she could do something like this to you?" I said.

"She wouldn't," Henry said. "She knows I'd do anything for her, and I'll always be there, right by her side."

"Yes, you'll be right by her side in court. But now, you do realize you'll be in separate prisons, right?"

The look he gave me was priceless. Although I still considered Henry a squirrelly little guy, I sort of felt sorry for him.

"Where did she get my scarf?" Uncle Bing asked me on the way home. "I never gave her one."

I shrugged. "Apparently, Ms. Landry carried it around with her everywhere she went," I said. "Delta said Henry found it in her tennis bag."

Uncle Bing smiled. "That's definitely something Bonita would have done. She was such a romantic."

My heart ached for my uncle. For the first time in his life, he'd been in love, and look what had happened.

"When Delta called Henry and told him what she'd done, he rushed right down to the tennis court to help the woman he loved. In fact, he's the one who actually tied the handkerchief around Ms. Landry's neck."

Uncle Bing shook his head. "That's just awful." The sad expression on his face told me volumes about how he felt toward Bonita Landry. For the first time in his life, I think he was in love.

Over the next few days, all the prisoners were transferred to more secure facilities, leaving the Gulfside jail open for new convicts. I teased Jerry about this, but he just shook his head and said he'd be happy if he never arrested anyone ever again.

We managed to hear the whole story from Henry, with only a few pieces of information being contradictory; but a lot of the problem was a difference in his warped perception. Delta was desperately in love with the idea of being noticed by other men, including Uncle Bing and Clyde Bullhouser, never mind the fact that she was married to Henry. Bonita Landry had everything Delta thought she wanted, and the only way to change that was to get rid of her, in Delta's mind. And her husband panicked, so he helped her cover her tracks, hoping she'd love him more because of it. But all it did was showcase his weakness, which Delta loathed. The only reason she'd married him was to cover her own guilty tracks, and Henry had incriminating information on her.

Clyde Bullhouser had to go to court for withholding information that was critical to the case. What was with these people? I wondered.

Gomer, a.k.a. Shark, went back to Tiffany and explained everything that had transpired. And she did exactly what I suspected she'd do: She welcomed him home with open arms.

Crestview Country Club Communities kept Tom Masterson on staff, but they transferred him to another club. In spite of what they'd discovered about his past, it was hard to find tennis pros who were willing to work for peanuts.

Then, the company chairman asked me to work with them on a freelance basis. "We've had such a difficult time with some of our communities, and we were hoping you might consider going in undercover to help us out," he said. "We can give you a two-year contract to investigate a few things we've had dangling for some time now."

At first, I turned them down, but the offer was pretty good, and I was still trying to "find myself," so I gave in and said I'd do it on a case-by-case basis rather than a long-term contract. They accepted my counter-offer.

Uncle Bing was thrilled at my new hero status. "I always knew you were the smartest detective in the South," he told me. "And now we get to travel all over to Crestview's other communities and solve all their crimes."

"We?" I asked, scrunching my nose. The thought of having Uncle Bing "helping" me solve crimes blanketed me with a feeling of dread. But he was so sweet, I didn't have the heart to tell him he wasn't part of the deal.

I'll do that later, I thought. Maybe after my next assignment.

One thing this whole experience taught me was that regardless of age and economic status, we all want the most important things in life: to love and be loved.